We can build our dungeons in the air,
And sit and cry the blues.
We can stomp across this world
With nails hammered through our shoes.
We can join that troubled chorus
Who criticise and accuse.
It don't matter much
We got nothing much to lose.
But this wonderful life
If you can find it
And when you find it
It's a wonderful thing that you bring
It's a wonderful, wonderful, wonderful thing.

Nick Cave – 'Wonderful Life'

To my wonderful wife Paula.
Thank you for your inspiration for life.

This novel is a work of fiction. The names, characters and incidents portrayed in it are the work of the author's imagination. Any resemblance to actual persons, living or dead, events or localities is entirely coincidental.

First published 2006

Pensadores Futuros

www.barca-only.com

British Library Cataloguing In Publication Data
A Record of this Publication is available
from the British Library

ISBN 1846853079
978-1-84685-307-4

First Published August 2006 by

Exposure Publishing, an imprint of Diggory Press,
Three Rivers, Minions, Liskeard, Cornwall, PL14 5LE, UK
WWW.DIGGORYPRESS.COM

Steve Kenning

La Hermandad del Noveno Noviembre

The Brotherhood of the Ninth of November

Prologue

The Spanish Civil War (1936-1939) was a bloody, divisive conflict that opened up enormous wounds in the psyche of the country. The following merciless, bloody purge actuated by the new leader, Generalissimo Franco merely exacerbated the deep-rooted scars on the minds of the people.

The dominance of the Caudillo, the single party, from 1939 to 1975, was as a result of Franco's ability to play off different Francoist power based "families" against each other, such as the Falangists or the Carlists, or the Opus Dei, whilst always controlling the military. Franco was not overtaken by ideology: he was very much a realist and was open to change. This explains why this dictatorship was able to survive after Franco's death in 1975. In fact, following his death, a bloodless passage to a wholly different kind of government took place: democracy. Particularly in the later years of the regime, the army became less interventionist and a new generation permeated Spanish society bringing with them modern and democratic tendencies.

The transformation from Francoism to democracy was in all likelihood desired by many towards the end of Franco's rule, although it was certainly not guaranteed. There were many people and organisations deeply scarred by the Franco regime and as the Generalissimo aged there was a great deal of plotting and manoeuvring in order to either develop a power base or to ensure personal wealth, or both, in the event of Franco's death. Those that had supported the Franco regime were best placed to benefit from the new society that would form in the aftermath of Franco's death. Such people had control over the financial and political institutions of the country. There was great uncertainty as to how the country would develop as a monarchy. Old scores would need to be settled although there was also the recognition that the world was a very different place in the 1970's and that Spain had the opportunity to move forward economically and politically into a world free from mistrust and recrimination. The future was there for the taking. The brave and the resourceful would prosper.

Chapter One

Power, knowledge and death

Influencia, conocimiento y muerte

We live in a knowledge society, where knowledge is recognised as a powerful thing. Knowledge provides an understanding and a basis from which to work. Some knowledge is more in the form of information. This kind of knowledge when placed in the hands of powerful people, can be particularly dangerous. Conversely, possessing knowledge about powerful people, if misplaced or misused, can lead to death.

July 30th 2005, 9.30 am – Carrer Ample, Borne, Barcelona

"The man is a complete swine. His mother must have brought him up in a sty. He is a pig, a pig, a pig!"
"Calm down Jordi, calm down. Antich and I will be right over. Then we can talk everything through."
Jordi Torras was a sick man. He was unable to move far without his wheel-chair as his legs didn't work. He had lost one with cancer and the other side of his body was stricken through a stroke. He was dying and he knew it. He had loved life and now, in his remaining months, he wanted to see as much of it as he could. The only way he could still do this was through his computer.
As he sat at the old, huge oak desk, that was perched in the centre of his large first floor apartment, he grimaced at the computer screen. The resolution was excellent on the large, top of the range Apple monitor. One of his few remaining friends, Jesus Antich, was looking at him through the computer screen.

"Vale. I am calm now. I wish I had thought things through more carefully yesterday when he contacted me. I could have kept all the documents here with me and given them to you later today. I panicked though. The bastard son of a sow scares me. I sent all the documents and files to the Correos this morning with Senora Bosch. I do not trust La Correos, they lose everything."
"Ahh, Jordi. Who is this Senora Bosch? Is she a new love in your life?" Antich was trying to lighten the mood.
"You idiot Jesus," snapped Torras with a smile.
"Do you really think that even my eighty year old housekeeper would be attracted by this face?" As he spoke he leant forward towards his web cam and pointed to his face. Antich laughed.
Torras returned to his earlier theme,
"That piece of hogs intestine knows that Santiago Lines was the only person who saw through him all those years ago. He was very astute and he made sure that he was as implicated as the rest of us in the actions of the brotherhood. Only Guell, Cots and I knew what Santiago thought and did. I am telling you now because, despite your dreadful goalkeeping, you have always been a good friend and a very safe pair of hands. …when he spoke to me last night he was very threatening….I am concerned that someone else knows the truth. You never know what that piece of….."
Antich, ignoring the last part of what Torres had just said, chuckled, and talked over the abuse coming from the mouth of his friend,
"I was a great goalkeeper, I just had some dreadful defenders in front of me."
"You were……oh, hold on, stay on line, there is someone at the door."

The huge oak desk filled the centre of the large apartment room. Wires trailed from all parts of the desk but they were all safely corralled into under floor channels. The several windows to the room were all partly shaded by heavy brown floor to ceiling curtains. There was nothing else in the room apart from a metal edged glass coffee table and two comfortable green armchairs for visitors. The room was prepared for ease of access for a wheelchair.

Torras moved towards the door to the apartment room, but he didn't get far. As he was half way across the wooden floor, two men came through the door. Both men were well groomed. The shorter one was red faced, stocky but looked very fit. His dark hair looked out of place and was almost certainly dyed. The tall one looked like a better built Cary Grant. Both men were in their late fifties or early sixties. The taller man addressed Jordi Torras in a firm, impatient tone.
"Jordi, you have some important documentation. We spoke about it yesterday. I said I was coming to collect it today. Do you have it ready?"
The two men stepped forward and now towered above Torras who was slumped in his wheelchair.
"Have you no manners? Do you always just walk into other people's apartments? Who do you think you are? Anyway, you are early, you said eleven." muttered Torras trying to appear calm and in a feeble attempt to stall them. "If you come back then I will have everything ready."
"Don't you dare waste my time you pathetic man." the Cary Grant look-a-like said.
"You know exactly what I want and I want it now!" As he spoke he leaned forward until his face was inches from the face of Jordi Torras.

Jesus Antich had briefly left his computer screen when Torras had gone to the door. He had heard shouting and returned to his screen. He could see nothing but could hear everything. He watched and listened intently. He knew the voice of the well-spoken visitor.

The two visitors stormed around the apartment turning over everything, looking for something that was obviously very important to them. At times they both flashed passed the web cam that was built into the computer screen. Antich recognised both of them. Jordi Torras knew what he was doing and he quickly, mentally planned the outcome of this unexpected visit. Slowly, as the two visitors were out of the main room, he positioned himself in front of the web cam.

It wasn't long before the two men returned to Torras.
"What have you done with the documents? Where are they?"
Jordi Torras smiled. He stared at the frantic look on the faces of the two men.
"I cannot believe that when I was younger I envied you…I wanted to be like you." He stopped and his smile hardened.
"But now, all I want to do is to be able to spit on you from heaven…when you are burning in hell." He started to laugh.
The face of the Cary Grant look-a-like was contorted with rage. Suddenly, he lost control and he raced at the helpless man in his wheelchair. The other shorter man tried to stop him but his efforts were half-hearted and too late. Jordi Torras was picked up like a rag doll and thrown in rage across the room. The taller visitor stood panting. His arms hung limply by the side of his body and twitched following the sudden exertion. He looked down at the crumpled wreck that was once Jordi Torras. There was no life left in the sick and damaged hulk. Blood started to trickle from a head wound caused as the body had hit the solid coffee table.

"I think.....he is dead," squirmed the smaller man. He paused, his brain churning, looking for a way out of this situation.

"We need to make it look natural....quick." The Cary Grant look-a-like clicked out of his solemn trance. Between them the men moved the body and wheelchair around to make the death look like an accident. Within a couple of minutes they had left the apartment, empty-handed but with a dark stain on their souls.

Jesus Antich stared for a few minutes at his screen. He was in a state of shock. He stared at the body of his friend Jordi Torras. He stared as the blood oozing from his head slowly created a modernistic pattern on the oak parquet floor. He stared as the realisation dawned on him that he had just witnessed a murder. The tears silently ran down his face. He made no sound. After a few minutes he had clarity in his mind. He saved the video feed and he arranged to meet his close friend and colleague, Josep Lluis Alvaro.

Chapter Two

Brotherhood

Hermandad

People come together, as a group for a wide variety of reasons. Sometimes they are forced together, sometimes it is by circumstance, but often it is by choice. Humans are inherently social animals and they feel happier, more secure and stronger in a group than they do individually. A brotherhood can be defined in several ways: It can be seen as the state or relationship of being brothers, or as a fellowship. A really precise definition is an association of men, such as a fraternity or union, united for common purposes. Or even a group of people where all the members are of the same profession or trade. Whatever the understanding of the meaning, FC La Llotja was definitely a brotherhood.

April 1975 - Can Pixho Restaurant, Barceloneta

FC La Llotja were having a very poor campaign. This was their 10th anniversary season and their worst so far. FC La Llotja had started life in 1965 as a social outlet for a group of young financial graduates during their first year working at La Llotja, the stock exchange in Barcelona. Barcelona was not the capital city of Spain, but it was the capital city of Catalonia, the industrial heart of Spain and, probably the most productive region agriculturally in the whole of Spain. So the stock exchange was important to the region, as were the careers that the members of La Llotja had embarked on, ranging from stockbrokers, analysts, and accountants to bondsmen. From amongst these young men some of the future financiers, industrialists and politicians of Catalonia would develop.

The future was in their hands.

FC Llotja played 10 to 20 friendly games each year against a wide selection of local opposition, ranging from the fishermen of the old port to the students of the University of Barcelona. Although the quality of the opposition varied immensely, from almost professional standard amateurs to scratch teams, each game was important, but equally so was the post-match meal and social. Over the past 10 years the team had fielded around 15 or 16 different players but now the original 12 players were the existing 12 players. The season was at the mid point and the team had not won one game, they had drawn two, but they had not really looked like winning a game. They had never gone a whole season without a win.

La Llotja was central to the Franco economy and central to life in Barcelona. La Llotja building had been on Carrer del Consolat de Mar since the 1300's and was part of everyday life. It was not that big but it was grand. The entrance to the building faced down the Avenida Marques de l'Argentera towards the Parc de la Ciutadella, and, being located alongside the port, it was near to the source of much of Barcelona's wealth. The players of La Llotja were all well bred and belonged to the Barcelonan middle classes. All were Francophiles and Castillians, although secretly they were all Catalonians in their hearts. Each was schooled mainly within the rule of Franco and knew of little else. Their lives had been ones of privilege and order. During Franco's rule there was great stability for the people who supported him and who ran the important government institutions. For these young men, life had been planned and relatively pleasant. However, all this was about to change.

A backroom in the Can Pixho chiringuito restaurant on El Suquet de L'Almirall in Barceloneta, perched on the sea front, was the regular post-match social point for the team. The restaurant could not have been placed closer to the sea without it being in danger of being washed away. From the outside the building looked like a very large shack, made up of wooden panels and corrugated roof panels, inside though, the building was transformed into an eatery of some class and real atmospheres. Here you found the very best seafood the port and the city could offer.

Inside the restaurant voices were raised as the wine flowed. Twelve men mostly in their early twenties were sat around a large table that filled the end of the restaurant nearest to the sea. The table was covered in several white tablecloths that overlapped each other to form one continuous cover. The walls of the room were covered in photos of people providing a living history of life in the area. Each year the full team picture of FC La Llotja had been carefully placed on the walls. The low ceiling, brown brick walls, and low level light gave the restaurant on that afternoon a deeply symbolic feel. The weather outside was poor and the wind was stirring up the sea that could be heard above the festivities roaring its disapproval. The conversation was also deteriorating. The usual exuberance of the post-match celebration was, as usual following a defeat, turning into a post-match mortem. The continuing string of defeats meant that the conversations were more gloomy and vitriolic than usual. Virtually everyone had a reason for the teams' poor performance and almost every reason invariably meant criticism of the goalkeeper, Jose Lluis Alvaro. There is a limit to one's tolerance and after about half an hour of this criticism he had had enough, "Vale, I have not been good this year…I have made mistakes… but how can I stop the goals with no defence..." At this point two of the defenders, Jose Baquero and Albert Cots, much the worse for vast quantities of red wine, leapt to their feet and berated Alvaro. With the two men shaking their fists across the table in unison at the goalkeeper, things were beginning to get out of control when the sound of a bottle smashing on brick silenced everyone. In an instance the hubbub of the room was closed off. The silence hung in the air. One man was left standing as the other players either sat down or rearranged themselves to get a better view of the excitement. The smashed bottle dripped red wine across the brown brick wall. The bottle had been half full and the full extent of the impact of the escaping red wine was revealed on the white tablecloth that stood only a few feet from the wall. It was if the whole room had turned in slow motion towards the source of the sound. Although within a few seconds there were 11 pairs of eyes on the 12th player.

Julian Solbes was standing with his right hand clutching the neck of a smashed bottle. For several moments no one spoke. Then Solbes, who was the team captain, and had been since the formation of the team, snarled at the rest of the players.

"Look at you, all of you. Nothing but blame, blame, blame. Take some responsibility. We are all to blame for our poor performances this year. Anyway, football is not life or death. But perhaps, the reason for our lack of success is."

He paused, looked disdainfully at his hand holding the smashed bottle before refocusing on his other hand that was holding a nearly full glass. He slowly took a drink from his glass and at the same time placed the remains of the broken bottle on the table. The other players were silent. Solbes was a man they all to a man totally respected. He was never a figure of fun and he was not someone you took on. They all listened. The atmosphere was so charged you could have lit a match and blown the restaurant across the Mediterranean to Sicily.

"Think about it." He paused, looking around at each man with real intensity, as if he expected him, in his drunken state, to really think.

"Franco is dying, we have all done well under his regime. We have all grown up under his rule. We know nothing else. In fact, many will look at us as being part of his regime. We do not know much about life during the Civil War but we do know that many people suffered and there will be people who have scores to settle. What do people think of us? We are rich. We are privileged. Just along the coast there are people living in squalor, in a shanty down, in Besos, in our city. This is wrong. We eat good food. We drink a lot, and then get upset by football. Some of these people are starving." He pointed north along the coast.

"How will these people react when Franco is dead? What will the unions and the communists do? We do not know what will happen once he is dead. I am worried about my future, in fact.....I am scared for me and my family's future. I am sure you all are too. We are living with this uncertainty on a day-to-day basis. I can see the fear in all of your faces." He stopped speaking and slowly looked into the eyes of each man. Most of them held his gaze, but one or two of them just looked at the floor.

"Yes. Some of you are terrified. It is no shame. We are living in a difficult time. Look at anyone you work with and look into their eyes. You will see their fear.........this is why we are so poor on the football field."

Several minutes passed while the other players thought about what had been said. The restaurant was silent. The sea was winning its victory. All you could hear was the pounding of the waves on the beach. The gloom of the room was supported by the sobering nature of the spoken words. Solbes stood for a while before he eventually sat down. At that point the other players muttered their agreement with his words. Within a few minutes normality was restored and the meal continued and the wine continued to flow.

Some twenty minutes later, Xavier Badia, a solicitor working for La Llotja, sensed the restored dynamic of the post-match festivity and stood up to address the team. He stood, glass of red wine in hand. The conversations around the table continued. Slightly embarrassed by his lack of impact, he cleared his throat loudly, held his glass high and announced:
"To FC La Llotja!"
With that statement the conversations quickly subsided and those that could stand, stood and raised their glasses.
"To FC La Llotja," they grumbled together incoherently, drinking the remains of their glasses and falling back into their chairs to a man. Badia took his chance to address them.
"Julian was right, we are all worried about the future, yet we are a strong team....we have a strong bond of friendship....perhaps we should look after our own interests...together we have the ability to protect ourselves and to provide an element of security..... perhaps we should ensure that we are safe and successful in the Spain after Franco. We are a very intelligent and influential group of people, together we can ensure our future, together we are strong, together we could act as a brotherhood." He quickly sat down, Badia was not a natural leader but he was a very clever man, he had sown a very important seed.

Chapter Three

Happiness, bliss and delight, in no particular order

Felicidad, dicha y placer, en ninguna orden particular

Someone once said that man could never be truly happy, as he would never ever know what his purpose in life would be. We are always searching for happiness, and although we often find pockets of it, something always comes along to spoil it. In a moment of self-contentment, sitting at a roadside table outside a bar, alongside a beach in high summer, gently sipping my third ice-cold cervesa, these were my idle thoughts and yes, I really was convinced that I had found the purpose of life.

July 29th 2005, late afternoon - Barceloneta

In fact, I was very close to real happiness, although I always knew that whenever I reached this state, which I had often done throughout my forty odd years of life, that I would still find a worry to pre-occupy me or I would become bored or discontented. The worries were often about my loved ones welfare or about a niggly pain I might have which was undoubtedly turning into a tumour, or about my capacity to spend money I didn't have. My boredom was often due to an extremely low threshold. My thoughts moved onto work, and I mused that I was often sublimely happy when I was fully engaged in my work, unable to find any time to worry about anything or find the time to get bored. This state always ended though. So, I thought, as humans, are we incapable of sustaining any feeling of happiness for a lengthy period of time? Do we lack the capacity or control in our brains to achieve true happiness.

"Charlie..Charlie….are you happy?"
The smiling voice of my wife, Kay, whispered in my ear. I married Kay two years ago, we'd been together for three years and worked together for about five years. We spent all out time together, which might seem potentially disastrous, but to see your partner in every aspect of their life, at work, at play, at rest, was, in my view, quite wonderful. It does obviously depend on the woman, I've had relationships with women which lasted much longer than they should, basically because we were only together for a few hours a day. When you have children a relationship is rarely the same again. Children put a strain on any relationship, particularly if there were weaknesses in the relationship. Sometimes you convince yourself that you are well suited to your mate, but when there are pressures, such as managing children, the cracks in a relationship become fissures. When you take time to look at people's relationships it is not hard to notice that many are often little more than a convenience, a partnership to help you get through life or to do the things you really want to do in life. Kay was my soul mate, my best friend, my equal and my work partner.
"You know the answer to that." I smirked.
How could I be anything other that happy with my life? I had a gorgeous younger wife, Kay was blonde, slim and 13 years younger than me, two lovely, blooming kids in their teens who loved Kay. I had a successful career, and a year ago we had bought an apartment in Barceloneta, a 100 metres from the beach.

The sun was particularly hot, local youths puttered past the café on their mopeds and the beer was still deliciously cold. I love the Mediterranean sun. That bright light that makes you squint. It was hot, but the cool breeze off the sea made it bearable to sit outside. Daquiri was our favourite bar. The bar area inside was very small and furnished by an odd, ill-assorted range of second hand kitsch furniture. It was a little bohemian, or so we thought, staffed and frequented by students and it made us feel a little younger. The bar was separated from the beach by a road and an esplanade. The road ran right outside the entrance to Daquiri and just on the first few metres of the esplanade there were seven or eight tables each covered with a different brightly covered plastic coated tablecloth. Kay was resting her head on my shoulder talking about how happy she was with her life. We were both teachers and we spent every available holiday in Spain, in Barcelona. It was the first day of our summer holiday and all we could see was another six weeks of relaxation and pure enjoyment, doing all the things we loved to do – eating, drinking, dancing and sun-bathing. We were experts at swanning about, and Barcelona is the perfect place for such actions. We fully deserved the break. For nine months of the year we work very hard in high-pressure jobs, then last summer we bought the apartment and had to spend an intensive couple of weeks doing the place up. As soon as we had finished we had to go back to England to work. So this holiday was our payback.

Horns started beeping a few yards along the road opposite. Two cars had slammed to a halt side by side. The driver of a red Fiat leapt out and pulled open the door of a deep blue sports coupe. He dragged out the driver and jostled him whilst hurling obscenities. Both men were in their fifties. The coupe driver started strutting as much as his assailant and pushed him away. Punches were thrown as a crowd gathered around the spectacle. It was far too hot for this kind of action. Both men were red in the face and sweating profusely. A woman in the sports car was trying to break up the scuffle. A young German also tried to separate them. The conflict petered out with the Fiat driver jumping into his car and speeding off. After a few yards he stopped and started to reverse towards the sports car. The crowd held its breath anticipating the inevitable crash. The red Fiat stopped a foot short of the other car and the drove off rapidly. The crowd went on their way. We were sitting at a bar, people watching – great fun!

Walking back towards our apartment from the beach, Kay and I were, very relaxed by the several beers we had each had over the past couple of hours, arm in arm, stumbling slowly along the narrow streets. It was about 5 p.m and still hot but the heat of the day had aroused all kind of warm smells. Barceloneta held a real fascination to us. The tall narrow streets ran in a grid system housing 4 or 5 storey apartment blocks. The apartments were small and the washing hung limply from the numerous small balconies. The streets were cool but oppressive at this time of year. The frictions of close cohabitation were everywhere – noise, music, arguments, laughter, TV, dogs howling – all these noises came together to give a warm feeling of community. Barceloneta, particularly in the summer, was a real mixture of Catalans, immigrants and foreign tourists. It was hell to find a parking space as every road led to the beach, but the place was vibrant.

After a few minutes we reached our apartment. The iron-gate like door was slightly open, which was unusual, so we took a few long strides up the two flights of stairs that led to our first floor apartment. We had looked at several apartments in all parts of Barcelona before deciding on this one, and an essential criterion for selection was being on the first or second floor. If the apartment block did not have a lift it was hell climbing up several flights of stairs, day after day. Kay opened the thick wooden door to the apartment. We walked in and dropped our bags. The apartment was very comfortable and we were rightly smug about how well we had renovated it. The light oak flooring and sleek furniture gave the apartment a really classy feeling. Even though it was small we had furnished it carefully and in a very minimalist style. We were delighted with our Catalan bolthole.

Kay flopped down on the small brown bed-sofa that covered one wall of the living room. I flicked on the cheap Spanish TV we had recently bought and joined her on the sofa. One reason for buying the apartment, apart from our love of Barcelona, and as an investment was the desire to learn Spanish. People in Barcelona spoke both Catalan and Castillian Spanish, but they all addressed you in Spanish if you made an attempt. We had been surprised and somewhat overjoyed, by the lack of English spoken in the city. We were quite poor speakers of Spanish and our personal development of the language was not helped by well meaning people speaking to you in English. We had spent a week last summer on the Costa del Sol although we could have been on the south coast of England judging by the amount of English spoken. Our Spanish was now rapidly improving, as it always does when you live in a place. Kay was particularly adept at the language, something she claims is due to studying Latin at school. We had developed our understanding of Spanish a great deal last year when searching for and buying our apartment. Kay would regularly phone a number chasing an apartment we had read of in the newspaper small ads. Sometimes this would lead to a viewing but more often that not we had to apologise for our poor Spanish and quickly retreat to our phrase book. When we moved in to the apartment we drove down from England with all our DIY gear and suffered a flat tyre. This necessitated a visit to a tyre garage. "Tiene una rueda para Mazda 6?" was eventually successful. Fortunately the Barcelonans are generally a very nice people, showing a tolerance and understanding to anyone who attempts to speak the language.

We were very lucky to come across an English estate agent and a really savvy English-speaking solicitor. The solicitor primarily dealt in company law with English and French companies and just took on one or two property conveyancies with English people just for his interest. Roma Bosch, our solicitor was an interesting person, with a fascinating name, and someone we had kept in touch with since the purchase of the apartment. He was in his early forties and very typical of the Spanish, business middle classes. Roma was a Catalan first and foremost. His love for F.C. Barcelona was highlighted by his semi-celebrity status as a historian for the club. He, like many Catalans, hated Spain. He would support F.C Barcelona only. He didn't support the Spanish national team or any other Spanish club team. Real Madrid was regarded as the white shirted *******.

The TV burbled with the kind of excitable Spanish that was ideal for us to get used to listening to the language. Kay rested her legs across my stomach and dozed off. I grabbed our latest restaurant guide and started to look for our next meal. We had gradually discovered wonderful Catalan eating houses, frequented by locals and which were extremely cheap. Our mission was to find more of these establishments. What really appealed to us about the city were not the tourist sites of the Ramblas or La Sagrada, but the culture of the real life Barcelonans. We would walk for hours in all areas of the city stopping off at bars and restaurants to sample the food, the beer, the wine and to soak up the culture. Such behaviour was to us pure delight.

Chapter Four

Brotherhood cemented

Hermadad cementada

A team or a group of people can be cemented together as a really effective and coherent unit by a number of things. When such factors include a real common purpose, a dynamic and inspirational leader, fear, or by a desire to make money, then the togetherness and success of the brotherhood is likely to be assured.

November 1975 - Can Pixho Restaurant, Barceloneta

Over the months following the April meeting of FC La Llotja, several meetings of the team were held. Each one of these meetings was to sort out the details of how the players in the team could help each other as part of the Brotherhood. The most important points for discussion were the need to keep the content of the meetings and the nature of the Brotherhood secret. Also, they discussed the need for some form of communication if a member was in desperate need. The Brotherhood decided to deal with success equitably. No one would gain more from the actions of the Brotherhood than any other. This was an area of real debate and conflict and nearly led to an early end of the Brotherhood.

The problems and disagreements that arose during these discussions were numerous. Eventually though, through compromise and camaraderie, the final details of the Brotherhood were finally confirmed at Casa Pixho on 9th November 1975.
"We are all agreed then, with this legal agreement to support each other in our business and family life.... in

every respect to ensure each of our personal well-being. Most importantly…." Xavier Badia paused and looked at the wooden floor of the restaurant that was littered with dead cigarette butts amongst the sawdust.

"Most importantly, we must make the most of the likely confusion that will follow the imminent death of Generalissimo Franco. There will almost certain to be a lengthy period of transition. We do not know what will happen. But we have the influence, the contacts and the Brotherhood to make all our financial futures very secure." Badia was wearing a black open necked shirt and a cream suit. All he needed was a pair of sunglasses and he would have looked like a young Mafioso. His face was red and the perspiration was building up on his forehead. He took a handkerchief out of his left pocket and wiped his forehead. He looked very serious as he prepared to continue to address the brotherhood. He was talking about a serious topic. He was talking about defrauding the government.

All the team had been party to discussions over the recent weeks about how they could utilise their combined roles to secretly and steadily, defraud the government over the coming years. It was important that everyone was equally involved and so, equally implicated. The responsibility was shared. Badia eventually continued to speak:

"We must remember at all times that we are only going to borrow the governments money. We must not be greedy and only use the money we need. Also, we must not talk about this outside this room." The men in the room were silent and solemn. They were about to play a very dangerous game.

"We all know what we have to do and when we are to fulfil our particular roles. Julian Solbes, Raul Martinez and Jordi Torres, have planned the detail perfectly and we have all discussed it several times. Is anyone in doubt about what we are to do?" Badia paused and gave all the men a chance to speak. No one did. They looked at Badia, together to a man. Complete in their brotherhood. The atmosphere was almost patriotic; it was silently fervent and very quiet.

The plan was to move money and other government funds around many times across government and related offices and organisations. Members of the Brotherhood worked in many different areas of La Llotja and other financially linked government offices. If the money were moved carefully and quickly in relatively small and usual amounts then it would be very difficult to trace. The money would be placed temporarily mainly in foreign government bonds before being used to purchase land and property. Details of the financial reserves of the brotherhood would be placed in one notary account in the name of F.C La Llotja.

"We will perform these activities for two years starting tomorrow. Then we must stop financial withdrawals from the government and very quickly find ways of returning the money. We will have a further couple of years to realise the benefits of the borrowed money. Whatever we invest in we must not touch the proceeds of our actions for thirty years, in order to avoid any suspicion. At the end of this period our investments will hopefully be substantial. We must guarantee to share our total financial accumulations with each member of the brotherhood exactly thirty years from this date. During the next thirty years we will rarely meet as a group and the team FC La Llotja will disband. Contact between members of the brotherhood involved in managing aspects of our investments will be co-ordinated through the office of FC La Llotja at Carrer Dispacio 121. This is actually an independent actuary who will maintain all records and bring them to our next meeting on the 9th November 2005. If there are any decisions to be made on the actions of any member of the team, ….all of the team will be involved in any decision made. If any member dies within this period of time we will ensure that his family receive his due benefits." With these words Xavier Badia sat down. There was a quiet gasp from the collective group. A few quiet conversations began as the men started to discuss their agreement with the statements that Badia had made. It had been a sober gathering, Julian Solbes though had stood up and walked over to a table at the back of the room. He picked up three bottles of cava and moved quickly back to the main table. Without speaking he opened each bottle in turn and passed the bottles around the table. Glasses were filled merrily and the mood of the room started to change. As this was happening Xavier Badia laid out the declaration of Brotherhood for signing by each of the team.

Julian Solbes had returned to his place poured him self a glass of cava, drank it in one gulp and then stood up again. As he rose slowly from his seat all the eleven other players followed him with their eyes. There was a significant pause. Then he spoke.
"We are all good friends…..but we all have seen how money can change people. For this reason we must protect ourselves against greed. The wealth we accumulate over the next couple of years will take many forms – bonds, money, shares and more - myself, Xavier and Raul Martinez will be responsible for putting all funds into property and land developments. All details will be held at Dispacio. For the next two years you must trust us to this task."
Solbes stopped speaking and looked at the brotherhood. Every man had him fixed in his eyes. There was no doubting their togetherness.

"We shall request an independent notary to allocate a secret number to the account, so that it remains undisturbed for thirty years. All deeds, documents and transactions will be kept in the account and all transactions managed by the notary. The number of the account will be made up of a secret twenty-four digit number that we will all be part of. Each of us will send any two numbers to Santiago Lines at the Notario on Disputacio. We must also send our team number to provide the order. Santiago, as you all know, is an old and trusted notary, who is as honest as they come. He will, with full knowledge of our dealings, manage the account until his death, which cannot be that far away. Following his death the account will remain untouched for thirty years until we all come together with our numbers. If anyone of us dies before 2005, we must send our secret two digit number to the person who is next on this team list." Solbes passed out twelve virtually identical team lists, each with a team number, a name next to each number and a current address.

"In case you die by accident you must make sure you have made arrangements for this number to be passed on." Then he paused and Solbes sat down slowly, but with intentional drama. The mood of the room was very sombre. Suddenly, Jose Baquero, a banker and right-half, shouted as he stood.

"Viva Franco. Viva La Hermandad." Everyone stood and toasted the new founded Brotherhood.

Chapter Five

Coincidences and very untypical incidents

Coincidencias y incidentes muy untypical

Sometimes things happen that are unexpected and which seem to link together for no apparent reason. When this kind of thing happens it is mildly disturbing whilst at the same time excitedly thought provoking.

July 30th 2005, 11 a.m - Barceloneta

I finished off my second cup of café con leche with a flourish. The sun was already high in the sky outside. I looked outside at the summer light and smiled.
"Are you ready Kay?" She obviously wasn't as she had a piece of croissant in her mouth and a cup of coffee in her hand.
"What's the hurry?" she gulped.
"Relax."
We were sitting on stools facing the three sided bar of our favourite café in Barceloneta. It was located on the corner of Carrer de la Maquinista and Carrer dels Pinzon, very near to the market that stood in the heart of this traditional Catalan barrio. The café was a real contradiction of styles, as it smelt, felt and looked typically Spanish but was called the New Orleans Tea and Coffee Company. The waitress, a young, plump, dark haired girl, knew me and Kay reasonably well. Whenever we were in Barcelona we went to the café for breakfast and we always had the same thing – café con leche, croissant and zuma de naranja – and the waitress knew what we wanted.

Half an hour later we were strolling towards the city centre, intent on a mornings shopping, probably along

Avinguda Portel de l'Angel, just off Placa de Catalunya. This street was a favourite with our daughter Susie, her loyalty was entirely due to a shop called Pimkie that sold fashionable clothes for teenage girls that were just a few months ahead of the fashions in Britain. Each visit to Barcelona without Susie resulted in a couple of clothes items picked up from Pimkie as a present for her.

Kay and I had just hurried across the Ronda del Litoral as the green man started to flash. The cars were moving well before the lights had changed to green, as they always did, making all pedestrians indecisive as to when to start to cross this busy road. This was a particularly congested area as virtually everyone going into and out of Barceloneta on foot passed along here. The correct route was wide and spacious but it did not connect with the places that people wanted to walk between. Everyone preferred to cross by the steps to the metro, which filled a corner pavement, and then walk single file, or in the road, along a very narrow pavement towards the city centre. We were just passing the entrance to Barceloneta Metro station as a crowd of people flooded onto the street from the underground stairway. Part of this group was a scruffy, casually dressed, young blonde haired man. He immediately picked us out from the throng of people that had just crossed the road. He eyed us and blurted out:
"Donde esta los Estacios Franca, por favor?" We understood what he said and we knew where the station he wanted was, but we both knew our Spanish wasn't good enough to give him directions, so Kay replied:
"No habla espanyol, somos Ingles." The blond haired guy smiled and said:
"Oh great…I'm Australian." We all laughed politely and Kay replied:
"OK then. We'll show you the way to the station…..it's only just down here.'

The three of us walked the 500 metres to Avenida Marques de l'Argentera before sending the Australian to the right along the wide road for a few more 100 metres towards his destination. During the walk he commented on how the day today felt very different to most other days. He had woken up feeling that something very special was going to happen. Kay had replied that Barcelona often felt like that to us.The city was on the edge, it was vibrant and spontaneous.

Free of the friendly Australian, we both stood on the next pedestrian crossing waiting for our chance to dash across the road on the signal of the green man. This road was a real challenge. The Avenida Marques de l'Argentera was a wide avenue with six lanes of traffic and numerous roads joining it at the point of the pedestrian crossing. It was always a relief to have crossed the road here unscathed.

"What about a walk around our favourite station." I mused to Kay.

"OK, we have plenty of time." she smiled in reply. We changed direction and walked in the footsteps of the Australian along the wide tree lined avenue towards the Estacion de Franca. On the way we passed the Park Hotel, a really trendy hotel which had been our base during our first visit to the city together a couple of years ago. The hotel faced the Estacion de Franca and a little way to the left was the Ciutadella Park – a lovely park that houses the building of the Catalonian Parliament.

The Estacio de Franca was, to be honest, only my favourite station. Kay liked it, but ever since I had studied railway station architecture as part of my Art 'A' level over twenty years ago, I had had an obsession with railway stations. As an example of railway station architecture, the Estacio de Franca, was, in my eyes, near perfect. Probably built in the 1920's/30's, it not only has a subtle feel of Art Deco but also one of former grandeur, although it is still in excellent, well-maintained, condition. It was no longer a major station in the city, with only a couple of trains leaving every hour, but the huge marble floored entrance and high ceilings draw you in as you enter and lead you towards the smooth edges of the multiple platforms and concave roof of the train station itself. Kay was used to me eulogising about the station and tolerated my obsession well.

After ten minutes of wandering around the station we decided on another coffee and headed for the station restaurant. Just at this moment a very portly man in his sixties, looking very much like a dark haired Spanish version of Alfred Hitchcock, was struggling up the few steps that led into the station concourse. He was red faced and clutching his arm. He collapsed at our feet. We both bent down instinctively to help him. The man was very well dressed and oozed of wealth. As he lay on the floor he struggled to get something out of his jacket pocket. I tried to help find what he was looking for.
"Aqui! Aqui!" he spluttered and forced my hand into his inside jacket pocket. I pulled out a wallet and a small white jar of tablets. The jar was empty. The man held my hand and stared me in the eyes.
"Gracias, gracias....mi hijo, esta mi hijo." The breathing of the man eased a little as he lay on the ground resting on one elbow, although still managing to hold my hand. By now station staff were racing over towards us. Before a station attendant got to us the man squeezed my hand and uttered:
"Por favor, ...esta mi hijo.....tiene esta," as he thrust his wallet into my hand. The station attendant rushed to the man and said something very fast and unintelligible to us. We both stepped back from the incident as more people

arrived and tried to administer some kind of first aid to the man. Soon a couple of people had the man on his back and were pumping his chest. Kay and I stood back and watched feeling helpless. It wasn't long before an ambulance arrived. It seemed pretty obvious to us that the man was dead as he was lifted on a stretcher into the back of the ambulance.

A small crowd had by now gathered around the incident. Kay and I gathered our thoughts and turned to leave the station concourse. We were trying to understand what he had said to us. Kay thought he had said:
"It is my son."

As we began to move away from the scene we realised we were looking at Nick Jones, someone we knew from England. In fact he lived two streets away from us in England and was involved, like me, in running boys football. The three of us were exchanging pleasantries at the top of the several rows of steps at the front of the station when there was a commotion amongst the gathered crowd. We looked up as a motorbike sped up outside the station and a youngish dark haired man, with a neat beard, raced up the steps towards us. He pushed me with his left hand and tried to grab the dead mans wallet from my right hand. I was momentarily shocked and staggered backwards. Nick Jones reacted quickly and jumped on the guy from behind and sent him sprawling across the marble floors. The crowd that had gathered around the dying man now raced over towards this new incident. A couple of men made a grab for the dark haired assailant. As they did so he struggled free and raced out of the station and leapt onto the back of the waiting motorbike. Kay, Nick and I stared in disbelief as the motorbike raced off along the avenue and around a corner and out of sight.

Kay was the first to speak as Nick and I dusted ourselves down:
"Are you two alright?"
We both nodded.
"What on earth was that all about?"
All three of us looked at the wallet in my hand. The wallet had been the target of the attack. What was so special about it? The wallet was full size and made of light brown calfskin. Embossed in gold letters was the name of what we presumed was the name of the dead man, Xavier Badia. I opened up the wallet. It was full of money, probably 2000 euros, mostly in fifty, euro notes. There were no credit or bankcards. The only other thing in the wallet was an old piece of paper with very old writing on it. The writing said: FC La Llotja and listed twelve names: Julian Solbes 8, Jesus Antich 6, Josep Lluis Alvaro 1, Xavier Badia 3, Salvador Camps 9, Manuel Perez 12, Raul Martinez 11, Rafael Gastesi 4, Jose Baquero 2, Albert Cots 5, Jordi Torras 7, Rafael Guell 10. The names of Albert Cots and Rafael Guell were crossed out and the rest had various different addresses written next to them. The three of us looked at the paper for a few minutes, then I folded it along its original folds and placed it carefully inside the wallet. The wallet was very soft and slid easily into the rear pocket of the long brown shorts I was wearing. Kay then guided us towards the station café where we could try to make some sense of what had happened over the past ten minutes.

Chapter Six

Just when life seems perfect.........

Apenas cuando la vida se parece perfecta.........

Life is a really strange concept. There are millions of people on this planet, all leading a very different experience and, every second, thinking very different thoughts. Each one of us on a regular basis questions the purpose of our life and ponders on the value of our contribution to this world. The redeeming feature of human life is, though, that we are all totally unique. Each and every one of us has a very different contribution to make, regardless of however pious or sanctimonious we are. I have come to realise that my life purpose is to make other people believe in themselves and, beyond that, to really enjoy myself. Despite this, sometimes things happen that really upset your equilibrium. Today was one of those days.

July 29th 2005, mid-day – Estacion de Franca, Barcelona

My double cortado was just beginning to have an impact. The caffeine was flowing through my veins and I was beginning to get a little manic.
"Calm down Charlie," Kay insisted, whilst holding my hand. Nick had left us a few minutes ago, as his train was about to leave. He could see no reason why I had just been jumped on by a bearded Spaniard.

"There has to be a connection with the old guy and the bearded attacker." I blurted, "There cannot be two strange coincidences like that in the space of a few minutes."
Kay was doing her calming bit to me.

"C'mon Charlie. Get real. There was this old guy who happened to fall dead at our feet and pass you a list of his mates. Then someone tried to mug you for the wallet you had in your hand. It's just a coincidence."
I wasn't convinced.
"People just aren't attacked in broad daylight in Barcelona – there has to be a reason….and anyway, why did the old man give me his wallet?"
Kay was by now beginning to get a little fed up with my manic insistence that I was the centre of some conspiratorial plot.
"Charles."
I knew she meant business when she called me Charles.
"Just stop it and let's move on. It has happened and that's it. Do you want another coffee……. I certainly do."
Without waiting for the reply she attracted the waiters attention and ordered another two coffees. It was obviously time to put our mind to other things.

Fifteen minutes later we had had a change of plan and were heading back to our apartment to get changed for the beach. The shopping trip could wait for another day. We both agreed that a couple of hours on the beach, followed by a couple of beers would re-focus our minds on relaxation. We retraced our steps along the Avenida Marques de l'Argentera and then on towards Barceloneta. As we hit Barceloneta we avoided the crowded main street, Passeig de Joan de Borbon, and headed straight into the grid of little streets along Carrer de Balboa.

Kay had been insistent that our thoughts moved on and tried to make conversation about other passing things. I had politely returned the conversation, but as with most things, I was irritatingly convinced I was right about the earlier incidents. Whatever, my mind was racing to join together the jigsaw of pieces surrounding the incidents that morning at the Estacion de Franca.

"Kay?"
I pondered for a second deciding if it was wise to return to the subject of the station incident.
"Do you sense we are being followed?"
We stopped outside a café, unfortunately named Café Fanny, leant on the glass window and slowly looked around. I knew Kay had sensed something a little earlier as she had gone into her ultra alert mode.
"Hmmm. Perhaps," she responded.
"Let's go and have a beer in the Vaso d'Oro."
She pointed to the bar just over the road. She led me into the bar. It was a busy, typically Spanish bar. The bar was long, covered in a wide variety of tapas and there was only room for people sitting on stools alongside the bar. The tapas here were varied and very tasty. We liked this bar as it was always full of Spanish people and the barman occasionally let us try a sample of the more unusual looking dishes.
"Yes, I did have a feeling of being followed, as soon as we left the café in the Estacion de Franca actually. Strange but I think you might be right about the old man dying and you being attacked not being coincidences." Kay mused.
"Let's just sit in this bar. Look ....those stools over there." She pointed to the far end of the bar, just round the bend and close to the door.
"If we sit there we can see out of the windows in the door and keep an eye on things." she explained. Kay led the way around the bar and sat on one of the stools. As she attracted the barman's attention to order a couple of beers, we both kept our eyes on the road outside. For a while there was just the usual traffic of people and vehicles obviously going about their normal business. Then after

about five minutes, and just as Kay and I were beginning to relax and think that our imaginations were getting over excited, we saw a man stop outside the bar on the other side of the road. He wasn't particularly suspicious other than the fact that we had both seen him walk past the windows of the bar a few times. He was in his thirties, with short dark hair and tanned. Despite his shades he seemed to be watching our bar. He was on his mobile phone to someone.

As we watched the man from the safety of inside the bar, he was soon joined by another man. At this point we knew that what had happened at the Estacio de Franca earlier that morning was not a coincidence. The second man outside the bar was the bearded man that had attacked me earlier.

"What is going on?" cried Kay with a nervous exasperation.

"Who are these guys and what are they following us for?"

We were both quite scared. We had gone from an extremely relaxed and very content mood to a tense and frightened feeling in a matter of hours.

"Let's go and ask them," I said bravely, not really meaning what I said.

"Good idea," replied Kay as she placed a five euro note on the bar for the beers and grabbed my hand, pulling me out of the doors of the bar. As we marched across the road towards the two men it was hard to tell who was more alarmed. My mind was racing considering all the possible outcomes of this forthcoming confrontation. I quickly replaying all the possible scenarios in my mind and tempting out all the likely reactions I could take to ensure our safety. At the same time the two men looked totally shocked and dumbstruck to see us walking straight towards them. Kay had a particularly fierce look on her face, which showed she meant business.

"Quisiera?" She blurted out as we stood in front of the two men. It took a little while for them to react. The non-bearded man looked very unsure of himself and kept glancing at the man with the beard. He quickly composed himself and replied:

"Are you English?"

"Yes," we replied in unison.

"My name is Jordi Badia. I apologise for jumping on you this morning." He said offering his hand to shake mine as an apology. As I shook his hand Kay, who had calmed down a little, asked:

"That is all very well but why are you following us as well?"

"That was my father who appeared to die in front of you this morning. I was following him. He has not been well ....in the head," the bearded man said pointing to his head, "My father stole the money in the wallet from me this morning and we were trying to find him. We saw him lying on the ground and you with the wallet in your hand and thought you had stolen it."

The explanation seemed to make some sense to me. There was a lot of money in the wallet and Jordi Badia certainly connected as a name with the name embossed on the wallet. I was about to hand over the wallet and its contents when Kay firmly stated:

"I can see what you are saying but I'm not sure I believe you. There is a lot of money in this wallet and I would be happier giving it over to the police to sort out. We need time to think about what to do. Give me your mobile number and we will phone you later." This was said with such directness and deliberation that the bearded man simply reached into his jacket pocket and gave Kay a card with his name and number on.

"Here," he said as he thrust the card into Kay's hand.

"It is important that you do not involve the police."

With that the two men walked off back towards the centre of Barcelona.

When the two men had disappeared around the corner I looked at Kay and hugged her. “Wow…..I didn’t realise how tough you could be…That was really impressive. I was terrified of you.”
Kay melted into my arms, all the exterior toughness rapidly disappearing. A tear appeared in the corner of her right eye. She quickly wiped it away.
“I didn’t like that at all.” she said.
“Yeah but you really gave them a strong message.” I replied.
“I’m not so sure.” she continued,
“I think he was lying.”
“Perhaps we should have just given him the wallet and then all this would have been over with.” I countered.
“Yes, perhaps we should. But something inside of me said no. Something was saying that that would be the wrong thing to do.” I nodded in silent agreement with Kay’s words.
“Lets have another beer,” I said as I guided her back inside the bar. We sat with a beer in front of us and Kay placed the card the bearded man had given her on the bar. The card was a business card with the pattern and colouring of the Catalan flag faintly filling all it’s background. In deep blue was the writing: Jordi Badia, Private Secretary to Julian Solbes, member of Partido Frente Popular de Catalunya and the Parliament de Catalunya. There was also a phone number, an e-mail address and a contact address.

Chapter Seven

Life can pass you by, or you can take the positive decision to make the most of it.

La vida puede pasarle cerca, o usted puede tomar la decisión positiva para hacer la mayor parte.

Too many people sit back and let life happen to them. They mind their own business, don't get involved in issues that don't directly impact on them and don't help anyone unless they are immediate family or friends. This kind of person often claims to just want a quiet life and to just be allowed to get on with it. The same kind of person though loves it when something unusual does happen to them. Not when it is happening, as this is often a very stressful time, but afterwards as it gives them a really good story to tell and it shows to others that they are really alive. There are other types of people who are keen to grab every inch of enjoyment and excitement out of their lives. Such people positively look for risk taking opportunities, when really it would often be much easier if they didn't. Kay and I wanted a peaceful, relaxing holiday, but we just couldn't resist the potential excitement of taking the incidents of that particular morning a little further.

July 29th 2005, 2p.m – Vaso d'Oro Cervesaria, Barceloneta

"Look, this Jordi guy must be quite respectable as he is secretary to a top politician in Catalonia." Kay reasoned.
"Mind you, politicians are not to be trusted." I loved it when Kay had these open arguments with herself.
"I think we should just let him have the wallet back. It really doesn't matter about the money. It would probably

only end up in a police station safe for a few months otherwise." I commented.
As I spoke I pulled the brown leather wallet out of my back pocket. It opened in my hands and the old piece of paper fell out onto the floor. I reached down from my stool to pick it up. The light somehow reflected a pattern on the paper as it lay on the ground. I sat upright and unfolded the paper. We both studied it carefully as I held it up to look at the embossed pattern. It was hard to see what the design was but it looked like some kind of crest. The paper was extremely old and quite tatty. It was a greyey, cream colour, having aged from the original white. The creases were quite recent though, as it appeared to have been untouched for sometime.

We both sat staring at the paper for several minutes. The writing was in ink and penned by a well-educated hand. The numbers we soon realised related to their shirt numbers in what we presumed was a football team, FC La Llotja. Two of the names were scribbled out in pencil. Also, lightly, and obviously more recently written, in pencil there were some other markings on the paper. All the names, apart from the two crossed out had a number, 1 to 26, written next to them. Xavier Badia had number 3 written next to his name, which was the same number as written in pen. Kay then noticed something quite interesting. Top of the list of name was Julian Solbes, number 8, and in pencil next to his name there was a number 10 and a star.
"Isn't that the name of the person on Jordi Badia's card," she questioned, positioning the business card in front of her again.
"Yes, it is.....Look."
Kay was right. This was a coincidence.
"Maybe as they played football together they remained friends?" I summised.

"Maybe," responded Kay.
"But don't you find all this interesting and just a little intriguing?"
"Call it female intuition or pure nosiness, but I am quite keen to find out a little more about this bit of paper. Why would someone keep an old piece of paper in their wallet with the names of a football team on it?" She continued.
"I would particularly like to find out a little more about Mr Badia and Mr Solbes, now that they have come into our lives."
I could see that Kay had our next couple of days mapped out. We both enjoyed finding things out, and the chance to learn a little more Spanish, discover a little more of the city and possibly meet some new Spaniards, whilst engaging in a little harmless research appealed greatly.
"Ok, I'll tell you what we could do." I started.
"To get this Jordi guy out of our life we will give him the wallet, money and paper back in an hour or so, but first, we will copy the paper so we can investigate things further in our own time.......what do you think?"
"Good idea." Kay replied with a hug.

Later in the afternoon we had arranged to meet Jordi Badia at a beach café to hand over the wallet. We were sitting on stainless steel chairs perched on the wooden decking, set right on the edge of the beach, watching out for Jordi Badia. It wasn't long after 3.30 p.m, the arranged meeting time, that he arrived on the back of a motor scooter. The same man he had been with outside the bar earlier was the driver. As the scooter stopped Jordi casually stepped off the back and walked over to us. He had seen us instantly and was soon sitting on the chair opposite us. The sun was particularly hot today and despite a gentle breeze off the sea Jordi was perspiring significantly. As he leaned forward placing his elbows on the stainless steel table he asked:

"Have you the wallet?"
I placed the wallet on the table. He picked it up, opened it, checked that the paper was there, ignored the money, then quickly closed the wallet.
"Thank you for your co-operation. Enjoy the rest of your holiday," with those words he got up, walked briskly to the motor scooter and sped off.
Kay looked at me and smiled. We were now both fascinated by this situation. Jordi was not at all frightening to us anymore, but there was obviously more to this situation than he had told us.
"Did you notice that his eyes only searched the wallet for the paper with the names on, he wasn't interested in the money at all?" I observed.
"Yes, so it proves he was lying about why he jumped you." replied Kay.
"Charlie, lets check the addresses on the piece of paper. Let's see if they exist."

We had made two copies of the piece of paper in the wallet. We had both thought it sensible to have a copy each. Kay got her copy out. My beer was empty and Kay's wasn't far off. I eyed the waitress a couple of tables away.
"Dos cervesas mas, por fa vor."
The sun was really gleaming at this point. It was probably 4 in the afternoon. The beach was well stocked with all sorts of Barcelonans. The young rich, the young not-so-rich and the older well-to-do types with nothing better to do. Another two beers were placed on the table by the waitress. A few sips later and we were both beginning to display signs of real bravado. Our conversation was full of dynamic actions we were about to make. In the event we sauntered off towards our apartment.
"We need a telephone book," said Kay as we walked off the beach and onto the promenade. I agreed.

"Let's pop into Daquiri and borrow their telephone directory." Kay said excitedly.

We walked past the bar and tried to take a seat inside near the rack where the various newspapers and directories were kept without being noticed. We were quite successful in achieving our aim. Kay picked up a telephone directory and flicked through the pages.
"Do you think all the names will be in here then Charlie?"
I wasn't at all sure, but I agreed. Kay placed the directory inside her towel and we left the bar. I was convinced that we would never be welcome in our favourite bar again.

As we walked down the street Kay pulled the directory out from inside the towel. She searched the alphabet to find the first name on the list as we walked along. Her finger stopped on the player number 1, Josep Lluis Alvaro. The address in the directory matched that on the paper.
"There does seem to be some kind of connection with real people and this piece of paper," remarked Kay.
"OK. Let's go and find out if there are real people involved then." I responded.
A few roads later and we were at Carrer Sant Miguel, and heading towards our apartment. The outside door to our apartment block was a metal door with a kind of rough metal mesh attached. The electronic locking system did not often work and so the door often opened without a key. As we arrived at the apartment block the door was open. We quickly passed the first floor and entered our apartment. As I opened the door to the apartment I quickly realised that someone else had been in there. We pushed open the entrance door. As we walked in we were horrified by what we saw. Our beautiful apartment was in total disarray. It wasn't a big apartment and there were not

many ornaments or other items apart from clothes and furniture in it.
"Oh my god." cried Kay.
"What has happened here?"
"Oh no." I said with my face in my hands.
"Why would someone do this? It looks like nothing has been taken. It can only be that someone thinks we have got some special information."

Chapter Eight

When the going gets tough the tough get going- or do they?

¿Cuándo el ir consigue resistente el resistente consigue que va o?

People often like to think that they would act heroically in the event of a crisis, being strong and standing up to danger and helping others. In reality very few of us ever face real danger and go through our lives secretly quite pleased that our bravery has not been tested. On the occasions it is tested people often surprise themselves with their previously unknown capacity to cope with whatever is thrown at them. People rarely lie down and play dead, they respond with raw human emotion and a desire to defend themselves.

July 29th 2005, 4.45 p.m - 1o1o, 104 Carrer Sant Miquel, Barceloneta

Kay and I were devastated for several minutes. Our beautiful apartment was in a total state of dishevelment. Nothing was broken or badly damaged but everything was out of place. I reacted as I always did in this kind of situation. I started to hurriedly clear things up whilst swearing abuse at some invisible being. Kay took a little longer to settle herself but I watched as the steely resolve returned gradually to her face. After several minutes we were both busy restoring the apartment to its usual tidy condition.
"Stop that swearing now. You only swear when you're frustrated." complained Kay. This was true, so I shut up.
"There is nothing missing because there isn't a lot here to take. Certainly nothing of any value." observed Kay.

"Yeah, I can only think it was to do with the other incidents today as burglars would have taken the TV and our leather jackets," I mused.
"Also, there are no signs of break in. They must have used a credit card on the front door.....we must remember to double lock that door."
Kay slumped on the bed. The apartment had taken 10 minutes to tidy.
"This must be to do with today's incidents," she stated.
"But it can't be Jordi who did this, as he has got what he wanted. There must be someone else after this information." she said pulling out the piece of paper containing the team names.
"I think you're right. This paper is more important than we think. Perhaps we should go to the police."
"And say what?" responded Kay.
"We have no idea what this is all about. Why don't we look into things a little more first. They might be trying to scare us off, but it's having exactly the opposite effect on me."
I loved Kay enormously, but she sometimes had this scarily determined look in her face, which I knew would probably lead us into trouble. Yet I also knew that we wouldn't rest until she had got what she considered to be a fair result.

A little while later, Kay was taking a shower, so I flicked on the TV. I passed over a number of channels before settling on a Spanish news channel. It was hard to understand what was being said, but it provided good practice in listening to the language. There was an item about a severe hailstorm that afternoon in Lleida, a fair sized town inland, which resulted in considerable damage being caused to cars by the golf ball like hail. The next story was obviously about a fairly famous man and his untimely death. The picture of the person on the screen looked vaguely familiar, although I didn't pay much attention, as I was too busy trying to translate in my mind the words of the last sentence the newsreader had said. Then a name rang out from the TV "....Xavier Badia....." Kay stepped into the room at this point with her towel wrapped around her.

"It's him, it's him." Kay shouted pointing to the picture on the TV.

"It's the guy who died this morning at the station." We continued to listen. It was obvious that the television news was reporting the death of a famous Barcelonan solicitor, a well-known local figure.

"So he really is dead then. Jordi was making out that his dad was faking it." It was obvious to me that Xavier Badia had really died that morning. If so maybe he really was convinced that his son was after the money and the paper with the names on had a real significance. We talked for sometime about the significance of the paper, convincing ourselves eventually that as Jordi wasn't at all interested in the money in the wallet, then the names on the paper must be somehow linked to enormous sums of money or some really important secret. The trouble was that we had absolutely no idea, not even an inkling of what mystery lay behind this strange piece of paper. Both of our minds were racing with possible scenarios. Perhaps the team was famous and the piece of paper was an original and so worth a lot of money? Had it been F.C Barcelona then perhaps, but neither of us had heard of F.C La Llotja. Or maybe the names were not real but codes for some kind of secret message? We were excited but, even by our own standards, we considered every possibility to be much too far-fetched.

By now it was just after 8 p.m in the evening. We were hungry and ready to hit the town. We were both slightly uncomfortable about venturing outside knowing that there

may be someone watching us but we were determined to take this thing further. The CD player blared away with our personal god, Nick Cave:
"….So bring it on, bring it on, every little tear, bring it on, bring it on, every useless fear, bring it on, bring it on, all your shattered dreams, and I'll scatter them into the sea….." We pulled the door to the apartment shut as we headed out into the street.

Carrer Sant Miguel was very busy. The couple of bars were full with people spilling out onto the streets. These were mainly local bars and the one closest to our apartment nearly always had a drunken fisherman outside nearly all day trying to sell a couple of fish, seemingly, to us, merely as an excuse to sit outside the bar and drink. Windows were open and TV sounds, music and dogs filled the air. We soon blended into the street activity and relaxed into the early evening atmosphere of expectation.

We headed into the city towards Borne, a really trendy, bohemian area that was quite touristy but had lots of bars and restaurants. Our target was La Paradeta, a restaurant on Caller Comercial. We had been to this restaurant once before and loved it. It was very different to anything you could find in England. The building itself was like a huge refectory with plenty of long tables a whole family could sit around. It was self-service and you even had to tidy your own plates away. What was different about it was that as you walked in there was a market stall of fish in front of you, containing an array of seafood from sardines to octopus. You selected what you wanted and the amount, paid for it and ordered a little salad and bread, and of course, a bottle of wine, and then waited for the fish to be cooked. It was difficult in here to hold a conversation until you had your food as you were constantly listening with one ear for your number to be called so you could collect your food. It was very atmospheric though.

It wasn't long before Kay and I were sitting at a table attacking an array of seafood – squid, whitebait, saltcod, mussels and more. We had opted for a bottle of red Penedes wine instead of our usual Rioja and all seemed fine. The restaurant was not too full yet as it was quite early, although you could sense it was getting busier.
"Ok, what shall we do tomorrow?" I queried.
"Shall we visit one or two of the people on the list and ask them what they know about the team list?"
"Good idea," choked Kay as a piece of whitebait went down the wrong way.
"Yeah, someone might then be able to explain what is going on." As the wine and the food were consumed we began to wonder whether today had simply been a dream, or had it really happened.

Chapter Nine

Life is short

La vida es corta

It's not until you face death that you realise how brief life is and how easily it can be snuffed out. Life is taken away from people so easily in films or in war, but in everyday life any death just brings great sadness and grief. All the more reason then, for enjoying life whilst you have it, and for bringing joy into the life of all you meet.

July 30th 2005, 9 a.m - 1º1º, 104 Carrer Sant Miquel, Barceloneta

The bed covers were on the floor and a sheet barely covered our naked bodies. I loved Kay's body. I lay there in the quarter light of the early morning and just ran my eyes over her curvaceous body. She was 35 years old but in very good shape. We ran and exercised at least three times a week, which not only kept us feeling good, it toned up our bodies. I placed my hand on her stomach and ran my fingers in a circle around her belly button. She stirred and turned over towards me.
"I love you." were her first words. These were her first words each and every morning and they seemed worth more each and every day. My standard reply was:
"I love you more." We hugged each other. Life was so good.

It wasn't long before we came back to reality. Slowly I dawned on me that we had had a very interesting day yesterday. At first it seemed like a dream. I looked at Kay and I knew she was thinking the same thing. This kind of telepathy often happened between us. "It did really

happen, didn't it?" I questioned, referring to yesterdays events.
"Yeah....I'm sure it did. What shall we do about it today?"
Kay was stretched out in the bed, making the most of the extra room she had manoeuvred during the night. I realised that I was perched on a narrow strip of bed with my left buttock hanging in free air.
"Hey, move over. I'm falling out." With that cry I thudded onto the floor as Kay gave me a friendly nudge. I leapt on top of her and hugged her again. Before long we were lying once again side-by-side laughing.
"It's quite exciting this Xavier Badia thing but I really don't want it to spoil our fun. If it becomes hard work we'll just forget it. Yeah?" snuggled Kay.
"OK, but I sense that it is going to be exciting." I countered.
"Anyway, nothing is going to get in the way of our morning coffee and croissant. Let's shower and go for a coffee."

Forty minutes on and we were strolling down Carrer Sant Miguel. A short time later we were in the New Orleans Tea and Coffee Company Café sitting on stools, sipping café con leche and nibbling chocolate croissants. It was a wonderfully bright morning and the air was very still. You could tell, even at ten in the morning, that it was going to be a really hot day. The air conditioning unit was chugging away at the back of the café but the waitresses were all already suffering from the growing heat. The café was full and we had been lucky to find a couple of stools. Kay opened up the telephone directory she had borrowed the night before and started to look up the names on the paper. She looked for each name and checked the addresses against those in the directory. If the addresses had changed she wrote down any alternatives. I was soon bored so I picked up a copy of the morning daily paper, El Periodico. This was published in Catalan and Castillian, fortunately the copy lying on the café bar was the Castillian version. I always preferred the other Catalan based newspaper, La Vanguardia, as it appeared a little more heavyweight, not that I understood a great deal, but I felt reading them helped my understanding of Spanish. I took a sip of my coffee as I slowly turned the pages of the newspaper trying to understand the headlines. Kay glanced over every few minutes, in between writing new addresses down from the telephone directory.

Page 8 was full of what seemed like an exciting incident where a light aircraft had missed the small airport on the edge of Barcelona and landed on a major road carriageway. I was trying to understand the gist of the story when Kay started to take a particular interest in another story on the page.
"Look at this story Charlie," she said pointing to a small paragraph.
"It says, I think, that a man was killed yesterday by a road tanker in Gracia."
"So? I'm sure that happens a lot." I replied disdainfully.
"Yes but Charlie, look," she insisted pointing to a line in the news report. Her finger ran underneath a name, 'Rafael Gastesi'.
"Do you see?" Kay asked.
"Look the name is on the list," her fingers moved over to the photocopy of the old piece of paper with the names on.
"Is it the same person?" I asked. We searched the news report for more details.
"Doesn't that say that it was a fifty-seven year old man and that bit, something about being a financier?" I gabbled. Kay was reading the address on the piece of paper.

"Yes, it must be him. He lives in Gracia."
"Let's look for something about the Xavier Badia death, I'd almost forgotten about it," I said as I turned back to the front of the paper. I started scrutinising each story. Kay was on my shoulder doing the same. There it was on page 2, quite a large article about him and his death from a suspected heart attack.

Kay ordered two more coffees and we continued to scan the paper. We were surprised to find a story about Julian Solbes, who Jordi Badia worked for and who was also a name on our list. The story was connected with Solbes' bid to become the President of the Catalonian Parliament, he was already the leader of the Partidia Popular, a very popular party in Barcelona and one of the main parties in Catalonia. Our eyes returned to the newspaper, searching the stories. On the final few pages we found a story about the unexpected death of a President of F.C Barcelona, Jose Baquero, who was found washed up on the beach fully clothed last night. It was suspected that he had fallen into the docks near the Maremagnum area of restaurants and nightclubs following a night of entertainment. He was another name on our list.
"Don't you think it's quite amazing that on the day we get handed a list of names that three of the names die?" questioned Kay.
"I really don't understand all this. It really is quite scary. All three were in their late fifties but it is a real coincidence that they died on the same day. Do you think they did die naturally, accidently or what?" I queried.
Kay was beginning to look very concerned.
"I really think that this is too much of a coincidence for all three deaths to be natural. It is probably very dangerous for us to get involved if their deaths are not natural. Maybe we should go to the police now."

"I think you're right but let's just check out one or two of the names and addresses today before we go to the police. If we are still convinced that something is going on we'll go to the police this evening. OK?" My words sounded more reasonable and braver than I felt. Why we were getting involved I didn't really know.
"Ok." agreed Kay.
"Let's look at the list and work out who is dead and who is alive." She pulled the list onto the bar right in front of us.
"So Albert Cots and Rafael Guell are already crossed out, presumed dead, but we need to check on these. Xavier Badia, team number 3 and pencil number 3, is dead. Jose Baquero, team number 2 and number 1 in pencil, and Rafael Gastesi, team number 4 and pencil number 2, were also dead.......so numbers 1, 2, and 3 in pencil are dead....Do you think we ought to check out number 4 next, just in case?"
The team sheet read: 1. Josep Lluis Alvaro (18 in pencil), 2. Jose Baquero (1), 3. Xavier Badia (13), 4. Rafael Gastesi (15), 5. Albert Cots (crossed out) (14), 6. Jesus Antich (20), 7. Jordi Torras (21), 8. Julian Solbes (10*), 9. Salvador Camps (18), 10. Rafael Guell (crossed out) (18), 11. Raul Martinez (15), 12. Manuel Perez (2*).
"I have to say," I started:
"That if they are being killed, with numbers 2, 3, 4 and 5 dead, the killer must really hate defenders."
"Charlie, you are sick sometimes."

We had decided in the café to seek out the person with number 4 written in pencil on the team sheet, Jordi Torras. His address was well within reach of the café on foot, 46 Carrer Ample, right in the heart of the Barri Gothic, the medieval heart of Barcelona.

We were soon walking amongst the tourists in front of the beautiful old church of Santa Maria del Mar. A labyrinth of narrow streets surrounded the church. At this time of the late morning shafts of light were allowed onto the pavements having fought their way down through the high storied ancient buildings that surrounded this area. This was a really special part of the city. The streets were just wide enough to take a car, but few ventured into this area. Streets and alleyways intermingled haphazardly having been laid out in the days before town planning. Kay and I loved the feel of these streets. The tourist flocked to the Picasso Museum, the Roman remains and the Cathedral, although far more enchanting buildings were to be found by mistake, by exploring any one of the many lonely alleys that lay off the tourist routes. Wandering these streets you could escape to any time, any era, and just let your mind imagine.

In stark contrast we soon hit Via Laietana, apparently named after the ancient tribe that once colonised these parts. This was an artificial artery sliced through the medieval quarter. We crossed the heaving traffic at a crossing and soon disappeared back into the alleyways. During our first visit to Barcelona we had discovered a very atmospheric restaurant called Pla that was along a side alley in this area. The afternoon we had come across the place we had instantly booked a table for the evening, only to be unable to find the place again without a great amount of difficulty, such were the intricacies of the layout of the Barri Gothic. This area chilled your spine and tingled your senses. It was rarely busy, and it was remote from the tourists, dark and an anonymous danger lurked behind every corner and along every alley. We loved it.

We eventually arrived at Carrer Ample and found an arched entrance that led to an inner entrance hall and number 46. Access to the inner hallway was through a very smart looking double glass doorway that was framed by some very fancy and decorative ironwork. On the wall to the right of the door there were four buttons and name plates. Three of the names were companies of various kinds, but the other had the name clearly printed in black, Jordi Torras. Kay pressed the buzzer. We waited for a voice on the intercom. Nothing. I pressed the buzzer again impatiently.

Chapter Ten

Déjà Vu

Déjà Vu

There are times in your life when you know that you have been in a certain place or in a similar situation before, even when you are convinced that you haven't. Such a feeling is almost like an additional sense. Déjà vu is particularly spooky when you know what is going to happen next or when you are sure about what you need to do next. As we stood outside number 46 Carrer Ample I had a really weird feeling that I knew this place.

July 30th 2005, 11.30 a.m – Carrer Ample, Borne, Barcelona

Kay was now getting impatient. She continued to ring the buzzer for several minutes. "No answer, no bloody answer! There must be some way in to see what this place is like."

"We can't break in, we just want to see who he is and if he knows anything about FC La Llotja," I said calmingly. Whilst I was speaking I had a feeling that I knew a way out of this situation.

"I am sure I know this place. I'm also sure that there is an old couple that act as caretakers to the place." I stepped back away from the door as I spoke. As I walked backwards I looked up at the building. The glass entrance was very recent. The building was very grand, probably the former home of some very wealthy merchant several hundred years ago. The ground floor was made up of a couple of shop fronts, with the large arched entrance wide enough to get a horse through. As the building grew higher more windows appeared. From this angle in the narrow street it was hard to make out the upper parts of the rendered building. Somehow I knew that I knew a great deal about this building, but how?

Kay was by now standing in front of the glass doorway with her hands on her hips obviously in deep thought about what to do next.

"Don't worry Kay. I'm sure someone will come along in a minute or two."

At that moment an elderly smiling woman arrived at the doorway. She was very typical of Spanish mamas. It is a fascinating fact to any observer of Spanish women that the generally gorgeous, curvaceous, lovely looking women in their twenties all generally turn into one of two types in their late thirties. The rich and genetically blessed women seem to maintain their sublime figures, although the majority of Spanish women, usually following childbirth, disappear into an unseen dimension for forty days and reappear with a transformed figure. This figure takes the form of a square body mass with two legs, two arms and a head. The additionally worrying thing is that the sense of style and dress sense also disappears. The lady that had arrived at the entrance was of this latter shape. She had a gold patterned dress and a black cardigan attached to her rectangular frame. Her hair was short and bleached gold on top of basic brown hair. Her gold framed glasses matched closely her gold necklace, heavy gold earrings and rings. She was little more than five feet tall.

"Buenas dias. Puedo ayudarle?"

Kay reacted as if surprised by this intrusion into her thoughts.

'Oh, si.....habla usted ingles? Queremos buscar Senor Torras."

"No habla usted ingles, pero consiguir Senor Torras para usted. Espere un momento." replied the elderly lady with a smile. She plunged a key into the glass door, opened it and quickly moved inside giving us a warm smile as she did so.

"I know where I know this place from." I mused.

"I have been here before."

"Look, at those bollards on the other side of the road, they jut out slightly." The road was hardly a road, it was more of an alley. The buildings were very irregular and bits of walls jutted out at various points.

"When I was last in Barcelona, some twenty years ago, we only came for a day. I remember going up to the old Olympic stadium, before it was modernised for the '92 Olympics, and I remember going to this permanent exhibition of Spanish houses…Poble Espanyol…I think it's still in Barcelona… I don't remember much else. But it all just came flooding back to me. Later in the day we had had a bottle of wine….white I think …I just didn't like red then. We were walking down this road as it was getting dark. I remember that we were totally immersed in our conversations when a horse came flying out of this doorway. The rider was in a hurry to get somewhere. Even then it was very unusual to have a horse in the city. It was such a shock that Clive, one of my friends, fell over and banged his head on that bollard sticking out of the pavement. It drew blood, but he was ok. The doorway was open, there were no glass doors, but I do remember it now. I had totally forgotten about it until this moment."

"Charlie, that's all you've been daydreaming about for the past 10 minutes. Did you see the old lady who came? She said she was going to get Jordi Torras for us."

Kay still had her hands on her hips, but was now pacing around expectantly.

"Oh no. Oh no." These cries came echoing out of the courtyard. The glass door flew open and the elderly lady clung to the door handle, ashen faced.

"Seniorita, seniorita...este terrible. Senor Torras es ferme." We were not sure of the language but we knew instantly that Jordi Torras was dead. The door closed and the lady disappeared, presumably to contact the police.

Kay and I looked at each other in some disbelief. It was obvious that we had one thought going through our heads simultaneously.
"What on earth was going on? What had we got ourselves involved in?"
"That's four people on the list dead in the past 24 hours. There is no way that is a coincidence," stated a disbelieving Kay.
We were both stunned. We looked at each other without any emotion in our faces. Kay looked drawn. Her usual lovely face was stark. After a few minutes our eyes met again.
"There isn't much for us to do other than wait here and tell the police all we know," I added as we both squatted with our backs to the wall facing the glass doorway.
"I know Charlie, we must. But....I just have this feeling that we are involved in this whether we like it or not. Just look at what has happened since yesterday."
"You might be right Kay, but come here, have a cuddle..." I put my arms around her, "...let's just see what the police say."

The church of Santa Maria del Mar is a gorgeous example, on the inside, of the kind of church that can turn a person religious. The architecture is typical of the gothic period and at anytime of the day the atmospherics inside the church are restful and spiritual even to an agnostic like me. The approach to the church is only via a maze of different small, narrow alleyways that spider out from the church in all directions. From where Kay and I waited the church was a minutes walk. We crouched silently as the church bells struck on the hour, the final ring was punctured by a police siren wailing in the early afternoon haze.

Within seconds a police car bearing the signage 'Mossos de la Esquadra' arrived stopping inches from us. Very quickly, an unmarked car drew up behind it. We didn't move. We watched the action as the two uniformed Mossos policemen and two detectives went in through the glass doors of the old building. Very shortly more police arrived and sealed off the area. A policeman came over to us and said something to us in very rapid Spanish. He obviously wanted us to move out of the area but we didn't understand a word of what he said. We were reluctant to go, as we wanted to speak to one of the detectives. Kay was trying to reason with the policeman but he was intent on shuttling us out of the way. Just at that moment, one of the detectives came back out through the glass door to the apartment building, closely followed by the old lady we had spoken to earlier. She pointed across towards us and the detective shouted to the policeman to stop pushing us away and to bring us to him.
"You are Inglish, si?"
We both nodded.
"I need to find out what know you of Senor Torras." Tiene I.D?"
The only thing we had on us was my diving licence and an electricity statement form for our apartment. The detective looked at these and made a note of our names and address. His tone softened.
"I need to speak to you, but not know." He gesticulated that he was occupied for the moment.
"Look, hay a wonderful bar… Bar Salvador on the next carrer…I meet you there in una hora. Entiende?" His English was good but unpractised. He sounded like an Englishmen who had lived abroad for twenty years or so.

We both nodded at his statement. With that positive reaction he turned and went back inside the building.

Neither of us were used to dealing with the police. Also, although we dealt with often serious, unexpected incidents in our everyday lives running a school, this was very different. At work we were the experts, managing any situation on our terms, using our experience in our environment. Here, in this world of intrigue and death, we were well out of our comfort zone.

It took us a few minutes to locate Bar Salvador. Bar Salvador was a hundred yards away from Jordi Torras' apartment, located on Carrer Canvis Nous.

Chapter Eleven

Reality strikes!

¡Huelgas de la realidad!

It is quite a nice feeling to get yourself immersed in something without it ever really feeling that it is actually real. You don't worry about the problems or issues, you just get on with enjoying the experience. Very occasionally though, reality strikes and all of a sudden you realise that you have got yourself involved in something very difficult to get out of, and quite possibly something that could prove to be costly to you in a number of ways. Kay and I had a sneaking feeling that this had just happened to us.

July 30th 2005, 12.30 p.m – Bar Salvador, Borne, Barcelona

Bar Salvador provides an excellent experience of the real Barcelona. It's now on the braver tourist route, however, despite its growing popularity with non-Catalonians it still gives an authentic flavour of a local bar that provides good quality regional food. There is not much to the place. It gives a good impression of a run down café. Sawdust on the floor, a high ceiling, a cracked marble floor covered with several very basic tables, wine barrels high up on the wall, enhanced by a couple of loud, very busy waiters shouting and barking instructions. The menu is delivered on a photocopied sheet of paper and is in Catalan. You have to guess the real flavour of the items on the menu, which is part of the fun. The bar is always full of local people eating the best value lunch menu. Kay and I just look at what they are eating and ask for the same. The meals are cheap but the wine is the cheapest we have come across in Barcelona, it is virtually free. Ask for un bottella de vino tinto de la casa and you get a bottle filled with pretty acceptable wine from a tap on the wall.

We were halfway through a bottle of red and slurping our way through some kind of rabbit and bean stew when a tall, slender middle aged man strode into the bar and looked around with an air of real confidence. He had a firm, determined look about him. His black suit was very crumpled and he looked very hot in his shirt and tie. He paused at the door for a few seconds and scanned the bar. His eyes processed everyone and everything quickly, before long he moved across the floor of the bar towards us.

"Senor y senora Lowson? Si?"

"Si."

"May I sit down?"

He waited for a positive response before he imposed himself on us.

He was obviously a policeman, although that was a view formed by the fact that we were sat here waiting for one. He looked nothing like a policeman. I looked at Kay quickly and I could tell from her expression that she, like me, instantly quite liked him. He was a little different to most police, if for no other reason that he was dressed like, and looked like, a middle-aged Bryan Ferry, the leader of Roxy Music, the 1970's glam rock band singer. He had a presence and a confidence. His smile showed that he enjoyed life and did not take things too seriously.

"Will Ferran."

He held out his right hand to shake first my hand, then Kay's.

"Detective, Mossos d'Esquadra."

His English was as good as ours.

"You speak extremely good English," observed Kay.

"My mother was born in Coventry. I have dual citizenship but I choose to live in Spain....for the culture."
He waved to the waiter for a bottle of water. He grabbed a spare chair, sat on it, leaning forward with his elbows on the edge of the table. He quickly got to the point.
"I have just come from the home of Jordi Torras. At first sight it appears that he slipped on a newly polished floor and as he fell, banged his temple on the edge of an oak table. He is dead."
He paused and looked at each of us in turn, searching out our expressions.
"Did either of you know him?" We reacted without any concern.
"Why then, were you trying to see such a man?"
There was an inquisitive suspicion in his voice. He waited in quiet anticipation for our response.

Kay and I had, earlier over lunch, decided to tell the police everything, mainly due to the simple fact that things were seemingly becoming out of our control.
Kay started:
"This is quite a long story, although it only started yesterday. I think you need to understand it all if you are to see our viewpoint."
For the next twenty minutes we explained to the detective all we had been through over the past two days and what we thought the implications were likely to be. Detective Ferran was hard faced during our explanation. His face gave nothing away. He did not smile. He hardly blinked. He just stared at each of us in turn. He looked straight into our eyes. His deep brown irises bore deep into our souls. He was penetrating our every thought. Occasionally he would ask a pointed question, but mostly he listened and analysed. When we had finished our tale we but fell silent for a few minutes, exhausted, not just from telling the tale

but from the depth of Detective Ferran's analysis of our characters and thoughts.

"Thank you for the information you have given me. I am a little concerned that you have been at the scene of two fatalities over the past two days, however it is obvious from meeting you, to me at least, that you did not kill the men. From your personalities I feel that you are incapable of such acts. However, I am often wrong." He laughed. "My judgement is not my strongest feature."
By this statement we knew that he did seriously believe that we were incapable of any bringing any kind of harm to anyone. He obviously felt a connection with us. He seemed to like us as much as we liked him.
"I agree that there seems to be a link with the names on the piece of paper. All I know about the information on the paper you have shown me, is that La Llotja used to be the site of the old Barcelona stock exchange and that Julian Solbes is a well respected, but ambitious politician. The names of the other men on the list I do not really know." Detective Ferran said charmingly.
"We don't feel at all safe though Detective. You seem to understand our situation, but we are still obviously involved. What can we do?" I asked.
"I feel that this is a complex case. There seems to be a number of different people involved but I really don't think they are that interested in you. I think you happened to be in the wrong place at the wrong time. However, if you need my help …just call me. Here is my card."
With that statement he gave Kay a card with his name and number on.
"I need your address and contact details as I may need to talk to you further. I would suggest that you have nothing more to do with FC Llotja and enjoy the rest of your holiday." Detective Ferran rose out of his chair, gulped down the rest of his water and headed for the door.

Kay and I watched him until the door closed behind him.
“Nice guy.” observed Kay.
“Yes, unusual for a detective. Not that I know many.”
I had been pleased with the response and attitude of Detective Ferran, although I felt quite deflated by the result.
“ I really am disappointed that we won’t find out more about FC Llotja, I was beginning to enjoy the adventure.’.
“Yeah, but we will enjoy ourselves just as much in the sun. C’mon, pay the bill lets get back to the beach.”
Kay grabbed my hand and pulled me from my seat and across the floor of the bar. Before we reached the door we paused at the waiters bar to pay the bill. Then we headed out into the afternoon world of the Barri Gothic.

A bottle of red wine at lunchtime always seems to be a good idea at the time. Afterwards though everything appears to be working in slow motion and, although the surreal perspective brought on by the wine is very relaxing, in the end your body does tire remarkably. In such a situation, the best thing to do in Barcelona following a lunchtime bottle of red is to sleep it off on the beach.

Fifteen minutes later we were on the beach. We had diverted on the way to make a quick stop at the apartment to get changed and to pick up our beach mats before finding a good spot on the beach. When we arrived there, although it was a hot day, the beach wasn’t too packed. We liked the San Miguel beach even though it was the most popular. There was a real wide range of people on it and there were plenty of bars nearby.

We settled down into a real slumber on the beach. The sun was high and hot and we were relaxed. It wasn’t long though before some shouting woke me. I stirred but saw that it didn't affect us and closed my eyes again. Kay though was much more observant. She had been woken by the shouting too.

"That guy must be an undercover policeman."

She said pointing towards a very unkempt looking guy in his early thirties. He was shouting across the beach towards a couple of guys, one African and one Spanish looking, who although standing quite a way from each other were obviously looking to steal bags and wallets. The undercover policeman continued to stand watching the two guys. After a few minutes one moved off towards to port whilst the other followed a few minutes later. Kay had been sure that the two men had been watching us, as was the undercover policeman. I laughed and shrugged off the absurdity of it all.

Chapter Twelve

Outside the comfort zone

Fuera de la zona de la comodidad

Kay and I live our life continually pushing ourselves and stretching ourselves. We like to be outside our comfort zones. Gradual improvement through a steady raising of the bar of expectations is generally good for you. However, sometimes you can take yourself way out of your comfort zone. Very occasionally you become so far outside your comfort zone, that you almost lose control.

July 30th 2005, 5 p.m – San Miguel Beach, Barceloneta

Five o'clock. We had had enough sun. We picked up our things off the beach and arm in arm began slowly inching our way back to the apartment. We nearly always took the easiest and most direct route back to the apartment. From the beach it was probably 250 paces. The sun was still hot. The temperature indicator on a nearby advertising board still showed 31 degrees, which was very hot for the late afternoon. Everyone was sluggish, although there was also the sense of some vibrancy as workers who had spent the afternoon relaxing inside began to set off for work or start to get involved in their work. The evenings between 6 and 10 p.m are very special times in Spain for the non-spanish. In most northern European countries it is a time when people generally wind down and go home, perhaps venture out to a bar or a pub, but in Spain, certainly in Barcelona, it is perhaps the busiest part of the day. The noise, the smells, the atmosphere is unlike any other. When the weather is good, the early evening acts as a mere warm-up for later events – or so it always seems.

We crossed the esplanade and started walking in the middle of the road that cut across several of the main cross-barrio roads of Barceloneta. It was good to get into the shade. Kay and I were laden with beach mats and books but still strolled arm in arm. We sauntered to the cross-section with Carrer San Miguel, our street. We turned towards the apartment with a view to relaxing and showering before hitting a restaurant an hour or so later. As we headed down the street, just outside our apartment we saw a BCNETA van with three workmen busy doing something to the road. BCNETA was a very efficient organisation that essentially was the city council. We had been very impressed with the efficiency of everything we had seen the council involved in. We both hardly glanced at the workmen as they were a regular feature of city life.

Kay stepped in front of me to walk single file along the pavement by the side of the area where the BCNETA men were working and I followed close behind her. When Kay was right outside the door to our apartment building one of the workman stood in front of her as she went to put the key in the door. At the same time the other two swept around behind me. All three wore loose white BCNETA disposable uniforms, dark glasses and white face dust masks. Kay was instantly alarmed and stepped back. I grabbed her shoulders.
"Don't worry. But do as we ask and you will not be hurt."
The man in front of Kay instructed us in jittery English. With a few swift and direct physical instructions from the two men behind us, we found ourselves sitting in the back of a BCNETA transit truck before we had time to think. We hadn't been bundled into the van, but we had been forcibly guided.
"Sientese."
One of the men barked as he climbed in the back of the van after us, gesturing with his hands for us to sit down.

Inside the van was unremarkable. We sat on one of the wooden benches that mirrored either side of the rear of the van. The two men who had forced into the van sat opposite us and surveyed us closely.

"Que esta?" pleaded Kay,

"What do you want with us?"

"Tenemos no dinero," I added in poor Spanish.

The faces of the two men were expressionless. Both looked typically Spanish, tall, wide and dark. Both had thick black moustaches and were in their thirties. Neither of them looked particularly cultured. They were obviously the hired heavies.

"Kay, let's try and stay calm. This is surely connected to that bloody piece of paper."

I tried to stay calm, but my heart was thumping sending my blood rapidly round my head.

"I know, I know, but a lot of people have been killed. I'm scared." whispered Kay.

The man driving the van had obviously heard us and could speak good English. He looked over his shoulder towards us and peered through the grill that separated the front and the back of the van. He was much older than the other two men and had thick greying hair and a surprisingly kindly face.

"You must not worry. You have my word that you are safe."

These words made us feel no better at all. I held Kay's hand in a tight grip and we sat in silence as the van moved on.

It occurred to me to try to kick the doors in and jump out of the van. The rear doors looked very flimsily locked. I soon discounted this as the two men were watching us relentlessly and there could be no guarantee of us both escaping.

The van moved slowly through the city traffic, stopping regularly at the many traffic lights. After several minutes the van stopped and one of the men got out. He was obviously opening a gate or a door as moments later the van moved forward. The rear doors opened and the man inside the van jumped out ahead of us. The driver of the van had also got out and was pulling the foldable metal door across the opening onto the street. The doors were very heavy and it looked like a difficult job. As Kay and I got out of the van we had a good view of where we were. It was pretty obvious to me that we were in Poble Nou. In fact the road looked like Carrer Ramon Llull. When we were scouting around for an apartment we had looked at most areas of Barcelona and we walked everywhere. We liked Poble Nou, the old industrial area to the north of the city centre along the coast. The area was now being marginally gentrified and regenerated as the hi-tech business centre of the city, although there were still many streets that revealed the areas industrial legacy. As we glanced outside onto the street through the now rapidly closing doorway we could see several old industrial buildings across a wide street. The buildings in this area were very varied and quite ramshackle.

The door eventually slammed shut as we heard the lock close. The three men gathered us together and led us up a flight of open metal stairs. At this stage I could only sense how Kay felt. She looked ok but we couldn't talk, as the men had separated us as we walked up the staircase. It is hard to know how you will react when faced with danger, but I was very surprised by my present outlook. I felt as if I was having an out of body experience. Nothing that was said or done to me felt very real, and I seemed to be watching everything from a distance.

The stairs went up two floors. At the top floor there was a vast open loft. It was a huge area empty of any machinery or of any furniture except two wooden backed chairs. The building must have been an old textile mill. It smelt of dye and cotton. The walls were made of bare brick, rusty metal sheets or dirty glass, in fairly even proportions. The floor was rough wooden boards and the ceiling was quite low.

The older man was obviously in charge. As we reached the centre of the large room we realised that the two heavies had remained near the staircase, whilst the older man was standing facing us in the middle of the room.
"Please sit down."
He said in perfect English, as he gestered us towards the two chairs in the centre of the room. We did as we were told.
"You will come to no harm if you do as we say. I am going to tie you up. Please do not try to escape – we will only have to catch you again and I may not then be able to guarantee your safety. I will be back within an hour. When I return you must be prepared to answer a few questions honestly. Otherwise I cannot guarantee your safety." he repeated.
Kay and I just did not know what to say in reply to the man. My earlier calm was rapidly disappearing. The older man then proceeded to tie our hands and legs to the chairs. Kay winced as he tightened the rope around her ankles. He then strode off to the staircase and just after he disappeared from sight, the staircase disappeared, obviously removed to make any escape difficult. Kay and I looked at each other mournfully.

Chapter Thirteen

Honesty pays

La honradez paga

Lies never work, certainly not for me. To lie effectively you have to either really not care about people or about yourself or you have got to be incredibly clever. Kay and I cared about people and ourselves and were not incredibly clever, so we didn't lie. Some people believe that their life is a lie. This is a particularly depressing view, because if it is why not do something about it?

July 30th 2005, 7.30 p.m – A disused factory loft, Poble Nou

Life was rapidly ebbing away, or that at least is the way it seemed to me and Kay. We had never had anything happen to us like this to test our relationship. We regularly had difficult situations at work, but they were easy to handle as they were on our terms in our environment. We were in control. This was totally different. We were not in control and the environment was decidedly unfriendly.

It was hot in the loft. Kay was just to my right and slightly in front of me. We both managed to manoeuvre our chairs so we could at least see each other.
"What are we going to do Kay?"
"I don't know. I'm sorry for suggesting we look into this thing for longer than we should have. We should have gone to the police straight away."
"Don't be silly. It was a joint decision. Anyway, the older guy looks truthful. He said we would be ok."

"I don't believe any of them.....I don't know what's going on and I really don't want to know anymore...I just want to go home." Kay was getting very frustrated. We didn't speak for a few minutes. I looked around the loft. It was very grey but in reasonably good condition. It must of only fairly recently been vacated. Time must have moved on. The sun was getting lower as the loft was now a little darker than when we arrived. Work had obviously stopped for the day in the streets outside as all that could now be heard was the occasional car racing by.

Our moods were changing by the second. The mellow light flooding into the loft was affecting our mood.
"I really love you Kay. You must know that whatever happens."
"I really love you too Charlie." Kay looked me in the eyes.
"I don't feel scared. I feel really calm. It's as if I know we will be alright."
"It's funny but I feel the same...I almost feel untouchable in this whole situation."
At that moment a loud scratching noise stopped our conversation. The stairs to the floor below were replaced and a head rose up from nowhere. Gradually a full body appeared, followed by another. The first body belonged to the older man who had been with us earlier. He had obviously showered and dressed more smartly. His hair was wet and he had a smart dark suit and a pale blue tie on. The other man was even older. His hair was grey and very thin. He too wore a smart dark suit and a blue tie. Both men exuded wealth and class.

"You are safe and no-one will touch you. Kay you are untouchable." Commented the man who had been one of our abductors; he had obviously heard the end of our conversation. Both men gently helped us out of our ropes and pulled up two chairs alongside us. Kay and I adjusted our arms and rubbed the areas on our arms and legs where the ropes had been tied.

The older man spoke again.

" I am very sorry for bringing you here. It was a very dangerous but very necessary thing to do. I hope you are not too scared and were not left in too much discomfort."

As he spoke he lit a cigarette and puffed on it gently.

"You two do not smoke."

He informed us correctly.

"Let me introduce myself…I am Jesus Antich…"

"And I am Josep Lluis Alvaro," butted in the other man.

Kay and I looked mystified. We had no idea why these two wealthy middle-aged men were telling us their names or why they had brought us to this place.

"Take a look at your piece of paper," instructed Alvaro.

Kay had handed a copy of the paper to the police but had kept a further copy for herself. She dug her fingers into the pocket at the front of her skirt. With two fingers she pulled out a copy of the paper. She unfolded it in front of me. We could both clearly see that these two men were two of the names on the team sheet of FC La Llotja.

"OK. What is all this about?" I blurted out, taking the words out of Kay's mouth.

"We will tell you all you need to know. First though we need to know exactly what you told the policeman, …Ferran? in Bar Salvador. Here have some water."

Antich passed a large bottle of water to Kay.

"Why should we tell you?" questioned Kay.

"You two are very nice people who have got involved in something serious and complex through no fault of your own. The only people that can make everything right for you in every respect are us."

Antich made a gesture with his hands to signify Alvaro and himself.

Kay looked at me quizzically. I gave her a reassuring smile.
"Ok we will tell you everything…but only because we have nothing to hide and because we are putting our trust in you."
With that we spent the next ten minutes telling the two men exactly what we had told the police. Everything.

Alvaro had not said much until know. He stood up slowly with a sigh and started to walk around the loft, hands in pocket.
"You are unfortunately involved in this situation and you will be until it comes to an end. We will protect you although because of the information you hold you are doubly safe."
"What information" I questioned,
"We know nothing."
"What do you mean 'doubly' safe?" asked Kay.
"You have something very important but even we do not know what it is. You two have something that, we, and others, know is very valuable but we don't know what it is. Whilst we believe that no one else knows what it is you are safe."
I looked at Kay and she looked at me mystified.
"We know nothing about FC La Llotja….what are you talking about?" asked Kay.
Alvaro continued,
"Your apartment has some kind of secret that will lead someone to a lot of money. So much money that some people are prepared to kill for it."
"Please tell us what is happening." I asked.
"We will protect you, do not worry," repeated Antich.
Alvaro took up the conversation.
"Yes. We were both players with FC La Llotja and we were part of a fraud involving the whole team and millions of pesetas. This happened many years ago."

Antich continued,
"We became suspicious of some members of the brotherhood and started to watch their actions through the use of private investigators. We have learnt, from watching people and looking into particular issues over the past fifteen years, most of the secrets of the organisation of the Brotherhood and a great deal about the money. We are both rich men so the money is unimportant to us, but we are keen to protect the interests of all the team. Despite our efforts, four of the team are already dead. We are very interested in the sudden escalation of activity. With several members of the Brotherhood being killed…and we know they were not accidents…..over the past few days, we felt we needed to act."
"You are both safe, as no-one, we believe, knows exactly what the secret is that you hold in your apartment. They also know that you don't know. The word is though that you two need to be kept alive in order to cash in the money. We don't believe that anyone knows how."
"How then do you know so much about what has happened so far?" queried an exasperated Kay.
Antich, who was sitting on a wooden chair in the middle of the loft, looked up and across at Alvaro. He sighed.
"I suppose there is no harm in you knowing something about the Brotherhood. But, listen, Alvaro and I feel very bad about the way we have treated you this afternoon. We have captured you and scared you, tied you up and questioned you. You are both professionals and nice people, ….we have treated you in a way in which you do not deserve…"
Alvaro butted in:
"Yes, we had to get you away from your apartment but in a dramatic way. We have to protect ourselves. But you were about to be picked up by another, far more unreasonable group."

"How do you know, and who? I spluttered.
All this was getting a little surreal.
Alvaro continued, "For the past 15 or so years we....." gesturing towards Antich ".....have employed three private detectives, virtually full time, to find out what the members of the Brotherhood are up to. One of our team had picked up information that another group of people wanted to pick you up and force you to tell them what you know...we got in first."
By this time Kay and I had entered, mentally, a different dimension. Yesterday we were getting ready to relax and sit on the beach for a couple of weeks, yet today we were involved in an unpleasant and complex ordeal. Everything, these two men were saying to us appeared unreal and very far-fetched. I knew Kay very well and I could read easily what she was thinking from her facial expressions. She, like me, was finding it extremely hard to believe the things we were being told. We were both sinking into despair. What was going on and what was going to happen to us.
Antich added: "so we are sorry for the way you have been treated. We will tell you all we know and return you to your apartment, with some protection, if you agree to come out with us to a very quiet restaurant we know....it is much more comfortable than this place. ...Yes?"
We had little choice, but we agreed to go with Alvaro and Antich. They had treated us badly and scared us to death, although they seemed genuinely gentle and very non-threatening.

Chapter Fourteen

Should we stay or should we go?

¿debemos permanecer o debemos nosotros ir?

The Clash were a great band in the seventies and eighties and their song "Should I stay or should I go" is a classic. Sometimes, you can get yourself into a very difficult situation and you have to make a decision to stay or not. As Kay and I walked into the Portes 7 restaurant we were simultaneously thinking whether or not we should make a run for it, or stick with the situation and see it through.

July 30th 2005, 10 p.m – Portes 7 Restaurant, Barcelona

When we thought about it though, which was difficult to do, with any clarity, in the circumstances, we both felt strangely quite secure in the hands of the two middle aged Spanish men, Alvaro and Antich, and their small entourage, and decided to make the most of their invitation to dinner. Kay was beginning to regain her natural composure. I had always been impressed by her inner strength. She had now had time to gather her thoughts and to come to terms with our situation. She would, I knew, have decided we were in a difficult situation but a clear head would give us a better chance of survival. Kay gave me strength. We were a really good team, especially in a crisis. I looked at her growing assurance and knew that we had to start controlling this situation.

The Portes 7 restaurant was one of the most popular in the whole of Barcelona, which was some feat considering the number of restaurants in the city. It was on the Avenida Marques de l'Argentera and always had a queue of people waiting to get in. You couldn't book in advance although Alvaro and Antich obviously had. We were clearly dealing with a couple of important and influential Barcelonans. I had, up to now, been feeling very much on the back foot, but the arrogance of wealth displayed by these two men, obviously believing that they could do anything they wanted to do, was beginning to stimulate my genes that were intolerant and resistant to privilege. I hated privilege and class, and the thought that these two quite elderly gentlemen held the belief that they had undue influence over other people began to annoy me immensely. So, by the time the four of us were sitting at a table at the back of the extensive restaurant Kay and I were ready for a fight regardless of the dangers.

The table we were sitting at was tucked away in a private alcove in this very traditional restaurant. It was obvious that we were not to be disturbed. A waiter quickly brought us water and red wine then we were left alone at some distance from the other diners. Kay was looking good despite the afternoons' events. I felt though, and Kay looked, like we had both just come off the beach. We looked very much out of place with the two well-dressed men.

"Ok tell us what is going on," I demanded with real bravado.

"I am pleased that you are regaining your confidence Senor Lowson. But you really don't need to worry or to compete with us. We are on your side."

"What is going on?" I asked again, forcibly.

Antich and Alvaro were like brothers, although they looked totally different. Antich was of medium height, nearly totally bald, with fine features, whereas Alvaro had a head of thick grey hair and looked younger than he probably actually was. What both the men had in common

were really kindly faces. They had wrinkles in the right places and not an edge of hardness in their features.
The two men stared at each other. It was difficult to tell which of them was the senior in terms of decision-making. They acted and spoke as one. On this occasion Antich spread his arms on the chairs either side of him and relaxed, whilst Alvaro answered the question. It was clear from Antich's reaction that this was going to be a lengthy explanation.
Alvaro shuffled himself around in his chair to get comfortable. He sipped his glass of red wine and put his elbows on the table. He leaned towards me and Kay.
"I really like you two people. We know from our research a great deal about you."
Kay and I looked at each other stunned by the fact that some kind of research had been conducted on our lives without our knowledge. Our mouths gaped open.
Alvaro continued, "The Brotherhood was formed by the original 12 players of FC La Llotja, a football club we all played for. We were unsure about what would happen after the death of Franco. We were worried about our families and so we formed the Brotherhood to try to legally borrow government money, some several million pesetas, to invest in property, during the period of turmoil we were sure would follow Franco's death. In the end we did very little that was illegal. We simply used our positions to divert funds to our best interests. All the profits, which were considerable, were to be held centrally for thirty years."

Antich, at this point shuffled his body and joined in, "The problem was that we were never a close knit group. We all agreed to the plan but there were several different factions, many of which live on today."
"What do you mean?' questioned Kay, beginning to get very interested in this story.

Alvaro took up the storytelling, "No-one trusted Solbes. He had been our captain, and he was a great leader of the team, but we did not trust him. He was always for himself. I tell a lie .... only Badia loves Solbes." Alvaro paused as if he had said too much.

Quickly Antich inserted, "The team was full of cliques. Me and Alvaro were one, for example."

Kay interrupted their flow, "Badia loved Solbes. We saw him die."

Antich looked with some care at Alvaro's expression that was void of any kind of meaning, until he nodded.

Antich replied, 'Xavier Badia is not dead. You will see."

Kay and I were dumbfounded. We had seen him die right in front of us at the Estacio de Franca. I held Kay's hand tightly.

"What do you mean?"

"You will see. Everything is not always as it first appears. Life can be a deception." Before Kay and I could push the issue further, Alvaro who had regained his composure carried on his account of the Brotherhood.

"It was not long though, after the money had been diverted that there was a certain amount of suspicious activity. The Brotherhood fell apart after the money was put into action. Financial dealings were managed on behalf of all of us by a couple of individuals. We were all trusting but also suspicious. A number of events that happened increased the level of suspicion. Six months after the last transaction was made Rafael Guell was arrested and later died. As a result of this some of the Brotherhood had real concerns, and a number of very close alliances developed in order to protect each other."

Alvaro sipped his wine, "Albert Cots was a very good friend of Guell and Jordi Torras, he and Torras visited the independent notary Santiago Lines who was overseeing the secret vault of FC La Llotja. Lines was very old but hated Franco, he had survived the civil war through friendship of the Guell family and Rafael Guell's father in particular."

From what Antich and Avaro were saying and from the intensity of the way they were speaking, it was pretty obvious that they didn't trust Solbes and Badia. Alvaro went on, "When Guell died Santiago Lines had suspicions about his death. He had been part of the Guell family and he felt wronged by the death of Rafael Guell. So when approached by Cots and Torras he agreed to move the details of the financial wealth of the Brotherhood, which was in the form, mostly, of property, and, after five years of Brotherhood activity, had already amounted to several million pesetas?"

Antich chipped in, "That was in the eighties, there has been a considerable amount of extra investment, so just imagine the wealth of the Brotherhood today!"

I was beginning to understand. It seemed as if the two men were almost cleansing their consciences by telling us all this information. It was obvious to me that they had told no one else about any of this. Kay had the same thoughts:

"It seems that this is the first you have told anyone about this…why us?"

Antich smiled wryly and glanced at Alvaro. They both burst out laughing. This continued for some minutes until they were both crying with laughter. Kay and I smiled at each other nervously, this was not the response we had expected.

Antich composed himself first.

"We do not enjoy being part of the Brotherhood, although we are forever entwined. The aim was to make each of us financially secure, but not to meet that often. As soon as we had all been involved in some of the early Brotherhood related financial mis-dealings we were ensnared as a lifetime member of the Brotherhood. There was no going back. The financial activities we were all involved in were not really illegal, but they were all wrong and would have put us all in trouble, even if it resulted in us just being discredited or being thrown out of our jobs…"

Alvaro added, "Everyone was implicated with the exception of Solbes and Badia who took very careful precautions to ensure that they kept their hands clean,"

"…yes" continued Antich, "…we were all involved and implicated. Anyway Solbes in particular was a nasty, still is, person and he started to insist on regular secret meetings of the Brotherhood. He turned it into some kind of quasi-religious sect, demanding that we performed various rituals which gradually got more and more perverse." He stopped speaking. The laughter of a few minutes ago had been replaced by a real solemnity.

"What kind of things went on," questioned Kay.

Alvaro helped out Antich who was by now struggling to find the words, "There were various sexual acts he made us perform…he was...is…a real pervert. He loved watching. We were all forced into doing certain things. Some enjoyed it, certainly when women were involved but we all had to do what he ordered. He had a power over us. If we did not do what he wanted we knew he could, and would, expose our financial dealings. He was linked to the Brotherhood but he had made sure that he could never be implicated."

"All this happened a very long time ago in the early years of the Brotherhood, but we vowed to get him back for the humiliation he imposed on people."

Antich recovered, "…we have been trying to find a way for years. We could never go to the police because those two bastards are too influential, Solbes and Badia. We had to get some real proof." He smiled again.

"I'm totally lost now. Why are you now in a position to get revenge?' I asked.

Antich and Alvaro leant back on their chairs simultaneously and smiled.

We all sat in silence for a few minutes. I was looking at Kay and she was looking at me. We were both trying to get our heads around what we had just been told. Antich and Alvaro looked at each other with confident smiles. Eventually, Antich resumed:
"It is very hard for you to understand. We know this. We also know that the Brotherhood is using you as a smokescreen to send any kind of investigation away from them. It has been greatly troubled by Xavier Badia's son Jordi, who I believe you have met. He is trying to expose Solbes for some reason."
"If you want to get back at Solbes why don't you encourage Jordi Badia?" asked Kay.
"For the simple reason that the boy is a liability. Always has been and always will be." said an indignant Antich. Alvaro nodded his agreement. Alvaro then led on with the words:
"Revenge is very sweet, particularly when it is unexpected. We have told you what we have told you, as we know you are friendly with Detective Ferran. You will not meet a better or more honest policeman in the whole of Catalonia. We know he likes you and will listen to what you have to say. He will then never give up until he gets the right result."
"But you haven't told us anything that will enable Ferran to arrest Solbes. What has he done? Where is the evidence?" I questioned.
"Quite," reacted Antich.
"But, Ferran will start to investigate and we will gradually open up the trail to Solbes." He smiled. "The funniest thing at the moment is that the Brotherhood think we are playing along with their little smokescreen game." He chuckled to himself. Alvaro spoke again:

"You see, you are safe, you are just being used by a number of different people to get a result."
Kay looked as confused as I felt. What was going on? I didn't believe these guys. They were far too self-assured and smug for my liking. Everything they had said sounded very plausible but also very unlikely.

Chapter Fifteen

The secret is out

El secreto está hacia fuera

A secret is a secret until someone privy to it tells all. Secrets are invariably spilt, as human nature is not noted for its loyalty or secrecy. The best approach is to have no secrets, as then there can be no surprises and no living under a shadow, forever looking over your shoulder, waiting for the secret to surface into general circulation.

July 30th 2005, 11.30 p.m – Portes 7 Restaurant, Barcelona

The restaurant was now very busy. The gentle hum of conversation filled the old building. Despite the growing population of the restaurant we were still left alone, slightly adrift from the life of the place. Antich was the first to speak.
"Let me tell you. We are very happy."
As he spoke he squeezed Alvaro's hand.
"We have been closely watching events connected to the Brotherhood for a couple of years. Then a few months ago as Solbes started to position himself for a move for the Presidency there was a flurry of activity around the Brotherhood. For years there had been nothing as people had distanced themselves from the Brotherhood. We were coming up to the end of the thirty-year agreement and some members of the Brotherhood were beginning to get agitated about the prospect of their share of the finances being released. Our investigations showed a few different groups of activity. Some were after their share of the money, but we also picked up that Solbes was taking action related to the Brotherhood to try to clear his path to

the Presidency. He wanted a completely empty wardrobe with no skeletons from the past."

Alvaro was staring at the floor.

"It is so sad. He is a man we all grew up with, who we socialised with and who we respected. How can someone have such little value for his friends and for human life. We are happy though because although we don't know everything, we have enough evidence to ruin Solbes and to get him put in prison for the rest of his life. He has done some terrible things. If anything happens to either of us this information will be immediately released onto the internet. It will ruin him."

"Why don't you release the evidence now?" questioned Kay.

"Because there is much more information to come. We have a wonderful piece of evidence that links him to the death of our very good friend Jordi Torras who, as you know, died earlier today. Things are just warming up."

"If he was your friend, you sound really happy." I said.

"Yes, you do and anyway, how have you heard of his death so quickly. It only happened a few hours ago?" added Kay.

Alvaro's face turned ashen and he spat out his words:

"Jordi Torras was a great, great friend of ours."

He paused, choking back his emotions.

"I was talking to him through IM this morning. He was an ill man. He could hardly move. Several months ago he lost a leg through cancer and he only had a few months, if that, to live as the disease had accelerated its hold on him. He passed his time on the computer. He had few friends other than us and no family."

He had relaxed his speech and his tone.

" This morning he was telling me about the contact he had had with Solbes the day before. Solbes had telephoned him demanding information about the Brotherhoods business transactions in the early years. Jordi wanted

Antich and myself to go to his apartment to meet with Solbes…for support. I was still talking to Jordi over the computer when Solbes arrived at his apartment early. What happened next was fully recorded on my computer as Jordi left his webcam on."

"So that is your evidence," Kay asked sensitively as Alvaro was now sobbing. Antich put his arm around his friends shoulder. He added:

"It is a terrible thing to see someone murdered, but even worse to see a friend murdered. You may think us callous for doing what we have done with you today, but we had had it planned and we owe it to Jordi Torras to get that sick, evil man Solbes."

"You must have other incriminating evidence then?" I queried.

"Yes we do. We know as much about the Brotherhood and what Solbes was concerned about as Jordi Torras did. And we have the papers that Solbes was after." Antich smiled.

We sat silently for a few minutes to let everyone regain their composure. I still don't understand why we are involved in all this," I asked.

"Well, what I am going to tell you is new to us. However, we believe that this may be part of the smokescreen created by some members of the Brotherhood. Alternatively, this may be true. We just don't know just yet. Yesterday, we both received an e-mail from Jordi Torras, either just before or just after he died. He told us the following: Santiago Lines had to find a really safe place for the monies belonging to the Brotherhood. He had to put it out of the reach of Solbes and Badia. He was very inventive. Cots owned property in Barceloneta, he had brought a number of small apartments as an investment. All the apartments were rented out and, all the blocks were managed by a maintenance company. Lines, as a Notary, knew that each apartment stated the name of the maintenance company in the ownership deeds. The Notary changed the maintenance contract number of one of Cots's apartments to a new original number that related to a security box held by a maintenance company. This was virtually impossible to trace, and it just wouldn't enter your head to even consider. Unfortunately, soon after this was done, Cots suddenly died, closely followed by the death of Santiago Lines. This left only Torras knowing what had happened."

"So why did some of the other members of the Brotherhood start to get involved in things round the same time?" Kay asked.

"Well," started Antich.

"No one else knew anything about what Lines had done, only Cots and Torras, but this activity coincided with the Brotherhood members getting older and after 25 years some were wanting to see evidence of their work, somehow word spread that there was nothing in the secret vault and that everything relating to the financial wealth of the Brotherhood had been moved. This created a lot of activity and developed a lot of mistrust. Word developed in a number of areas that the apartment at Carrer Sant Miguel 104, 1.1, had the answer. No-one though knows why the apartment is important. Even we didn't know until yesterday."

"Why then are we so important?" Kay and I understood much of what had been said, but we couldn't see the link.

"You are very, very important. Only the owners or trustees of the apartment can gain access to the security box held by the maintenance company. Not even the police have the right to access it. You brought the apartment before anyone knew about the importance of the apartment....remember, this information has only really come to light over the past six months. Only Torras knew, and he had lost interest and a lot of hope after Cots and Lines died. He had no family and few friends."

Kay and I looked at each other. We were both thinking that these guys were being exceedingly nice to us and revealing all to us in order to gain access to the security box.

Antich was watching us.

"You think we only want you for the money. Remember, we are both very rich men. We do not want the money. We want Solbes. It is important to us that the security box stays where it is."

Chapter Sixteen

Window dressing

Preparación de ventana

Things are put in the shop window for people to see. Shop windows are well visited and eventually the person who really needs to see the item eventually sees it.

July 30th 2005, 11.30 p.m – Portes 7 Restaurant, Barcelona

Kay and I suddenly had an uncomfortable feeling. People in the restaurant had noticed us. The occasional person would walk past now to the toilets as the waiters had relaxed their control of the area. The conversation had lulled between the four of us. Antich and Alvaro were obviously pleased with their evenings work and seemed to want the restaurant to notice us.

"You seem to be putting us on show now, why?" I asked bravely.

"We have told you all we know but others need to think that we know everything you know," replied Alvaro.

These guys were clever. It did seem though that their motives were honourable…they simply wanted to get Julian Solbes.

Antich added, "Stay, enjoy the rest of the meal….we are paying. We will keep an eye on you. You will be safe. Feel free to tell the police all you know, but only Detective Will Ferran. He is independent, he is owned by no-one."

"We will be in touch soon," said Antich.

"We won't force you, but please think carefully about whether or not you want to take us to the secret security box. If you do we would make sure all that the financial

resources of the Brotherhood are distributed fairly or to charity. We are not keen on a big media profile…we have something to lose too."
With that the two men got up from the table shook my hand, kissed Kay on both cheeks and headed for the front door of the restaurant. Kay and I watched as the two men slowly worked their way through the now busy restaurant, occasionally stopping to speak to people they knew.

"Phew, what do you think about all that?" asked Kay.
"Quite incredible and unbelievable." I replied. We both looked very tired, very grubby and totally out of place amongst the well dressed clientele of the restaurant.
"Look, I really don't feel comfortable here. Let's go and have a drink somewhere quiet. Perhaps Bar Colombo just at the far end of the Marina. It's not far and it's usually quiet."
We quickly left the restaurant by the side entrance. We may have been followed, but we didn't really care. We felt fairly safe after the conversation with Antich and Alvaro. We hurried across the wide pavements at the side of the Port Vell marina, along the Passeig de Joan de Borbon. The light of the day had long disappeared, it must have been about 11.30 p.m. Before long we arrived at Bar Colombo. The frontage looks modern and lacking in character. The bar itself is nothing fancy but has a really good atmosphere. We opened the glass door and stepped down into the bar. The place was half full, as usual, with a wide range of Spaniards. Two empty stools invited us to sit at the bar. The usual barman, with his leather trousers and ageing rocker moustache, served us two beers. If anyone had followed us from the restaurant, they had stayed outside.

I sipped the beer, Cruzcampo. "Mmmmm."

I looked into the amber beer and ruminated for a few seconds.
"This is getting fascinating. I was really scared this afternoon, but now……I do feel safe. I think the fact that we are needed helps us greatly."
"Yes, but what happens to us after the security box is opened. Are we safe then?" queried Kay.
"I think we should get in touch with Detective Ferran straight away and tell him what we know."
"You're right as usual," I replied with a loving smile, "Let's just relax a little now and do it tomorrow."
Kay agreed and we sat in the bar slowly drinking and talking about each other for the next couple of hours. It was as if we had just met for the first time.

It was a busy summer night in Barcelona. The air outside was still and dark, the air conditioner above the door in Bar Colombo was working hard and displayed a very distinctive regular rattle. It was a peaceful scene in the bar. No-one was animated but there was a gentle hum of conversation. The atmosphere was calm and relaxed. Outside despite the stillness of the air there was a lot of movement – people walking up and down the Passeig Joan d'Borbon, either visiting the many bars and restaurants or heading towards the city centre for the late evening. Cars were numerous and noisy and there was a flurry of police and ambulance alarms heading off into the distance.

In the bar Kay stroked her feet against my legs as we sat on the high stools next to the bar. We had quickly drunk a few beers and were feeling very relaxed despite the ordeal of the day. The shock and adrenalin flows of earlier in the day had left us both very tired. Coupled with the alcohol we both felt very light headed, a condition that helped us to view the events of the day from a distance. The barman placed a small dish of olives in front of us on the bar. Kay nibbled at them.

"This really is a very strange experience. It just doesn't seem very real although there are a lot of people involved and it is obviously serious stuff."

"Yeah, I know what you mean. I just can't get my head around it all. I do think that enough is enough though. We'll get in touch with Detective Ferran first thing in the morning. I think we take him to the security box, then it's all over." I replied.

Kay smiled a very tired smile and rested her head on my shoulder.

"C'mon you. Let's go home."

With that we left a few euros for our beers and slowly walked out of the bar. It was still busy outside so we crept through the night towards our apartment and bed.

Chapter Seventeen

The ceiling of the world falls in

El techo del mundo cae adentro

Life is very strange. Nothing is certain and nothing is ever as it seems. Just when you feel slightly in control of your life something happens to really throw everything off kilter. Sometimes this is nothing more than a slight setback and holds you up for a few minutes while you get your head sorted. Very occasionally though an incident occurs that genuinely surprises you and sends your mind reeling.

July 31st 2005, 8 a.m - 1º1º, 104 Carrer Sant Miquel, Barceloneta

I awoke suddenly. For several minutes I really didn't know where I was. The dark curtains, shutters and narrowness of the street outside, always kept out the sunlight making it difficult to tell the time of day. Gradually, my eyes became accustomed to the half-light and I began to familiarise myself with our apartment bedroom. I couldn't remember how we had got into bed the night before and our clothes were strewn all over the bedroom floor. Kay was still asleep next to me. I stroked her head. Suddenly there was a sudden rapping on the door to the apartment. The noise startled me.
"Hola! Holà! Open up."
The noise had not only made me jump but had also woken Kay up.
"What....what?" she stuttered.
We both hurried out of bed and threw on some clothes. The banging and shouting was still going on.
"Vale, vale, vengo!"

"Who is it?'
I called sleepily as I moved down the narrow hallway.
"Detective Ferran."
That it was Ferran surprised me as it was very early and I couldn't work out in my mind how he had got past the apartment entrance without a key. Kay had quickly woken up and she was beginning to think clearly.
"How did you get into the apartment block?"
"It was open....look if you don't believe it is me look outside your window. You will see my police car."
We peered out the window and just below the apartment was a Mossos police car with a uniformed officer sitting at the wheel. I pulled back the bolt on the door and let Detective Ferran into the apartment. It was very narrow in the hall so Kay and I stepped back in to the living room and invited Detective Ferran to sit down. He followed us into the room and sat on the brown sofa.

Dectective Ferran had obviously had a hard night. He looked as if he hadn't slept for a couple of days. His suit was crumpled, even more so than the last time we had seen him, he was unshaven and his black hair was lank and greasy. He looked pale and exhausted. He leaned forward on the sofa and rested his elbows on his knees. He looked up at us.
"Did you eat with two wealthy Spaniards last night, Josep Lluis Alvaro and Jesus Antich?"
"Yes, but not out of choice," revealed Kay.
"What do you mean?"
"It was a very strange experience. We were forced into a van by them and their men yesterday afternoon and taken to a building in Poble Nou. At least we think it was Poble Nou. They treated us pretty well, although we were both very scared. Then, in the evening they took us to an expensive restaurant and told us all about FC La Llotja

and what they called the Brotherhood. They basically told us their version of what was going on," I revealed.

Detective Ferran looked at us disbelievingly.
"At what time did you leave the restaurant and where did you go? Were the two men with you when you left?"
His face was void of any warmth, care or friendship. He had questions to ask and he was focussed on getting the results he wanted.
Kay was getting agitated.
"We have just told you that we were abducted yesterday and you ignore that and continue with your accusatory line of questioning…why?"
Detective Ferran looked a little taken aback. He composed himself and softened his look. Colour of a kind slowly returned to his face as he relaxed a little.
"I apologise if I appear aggressive. I have slept little and I need to investigate this. I will explain everything later. Please answer my questions first."
Kay and I looked at each other and silently nodded in agreement to each other.
"OK." said Kay.
As far as we know we left the restaurant at around eleven thirty, it was well after dark. But Alvaro and Antich had left fifteen minutes earlier. We walked across to Bar Colombo and we must have been there for about an hour."
Ferran looked across to me. I nodded, sanctioning Kay's words.
"Yes, other people in the restaurant do say that you two were left behind for up to half an hour after the two men left. However, I do need to go and check on Bar Colombo."
With that Detective Ferran got up to leave.
"What's going on?" I asked.
"Don't worry. Stay here I will return shortly. The officer will remain outside to make sure you don't leave."

With that he left the apartment.
Kay and I were stunned. We had no idea what was going on or why we were obviously under suspicion. We felt frightened with the thought that we might be arrested. We were getting very used to this flood of adrenalin that kept filling our veins with fear.

"Do you want a coffee?"
Kay asked after a few minutes of silent torpor. I walked over to the window and checked that the policeman was still there, he was.
"Yes, thanks," I replied.
We both went into our small kitchen and Kay prepared the filter coffee machine. As the machine started to gurgle and boil we looked at each other with wide eyes. "What is going on?" asked Kay.
"It just gets worse and worse."
I poured milk into two mugs.
"Don't worry. We have done nothing wrong. We will be fine." I said without conviction.
The coffee was quick to boil. Kay poured it into the mugs. We took the steaming coffee and sat at the table in the living room. The coffee tasted good and the caffeine hit home, waking us from our drowsiness and cleareing our heads.
"Something must have happened. How did Ferran know we were with Antich and Alvaro last night?" I questioned.
"Lots of people saw us there last night" Kay responded, "Perhaps he is just trying to find out why we were talking to such prominent men."
At that moment we heard someone stamping up the stairs to the apartment. Our apartment door had obviously been left ajar, as the sound was very loud. We looked towards the small hallway. Detective Ferran soon appeared, sweating profusely. He really looked in need of some

sleep, a shower and a set of clean clothes in that order. He sat down on the sofa and regained his breath.

"Ok, Ok. I am happy with your alibi. The barman at Bar Colombo does remember you well. You are pretty much regulars there, si?" he stated.
"Our alibi?" stirred Kay.
"What have we done?"
"Nothing, I believe', responded the detective.
"Last night Senor Alvaro and Senor Antich, well respected and well known Catalan figures, and very nice men….I know from personal experience….they were killed shortly after meeting with you at the restaurant in a car crash on the Ronda Litoral heading towards Besos.."
We were stunned. I looked at Ferran with my mouth wide open and Kay fell backwards against the sofa backrest. We hadn't liked the way that Antich and Alvero had treated us yesterday, but we recognised that they were basically honourable and nice men. They also promised us protection. A particularly ironic commitment, as they could not even protect themselves.
"That is terrible," said Kay.
"How did it happen?" I asked.
"I do not believe that it was an accident. The breaks failed and the car wouldn't stop and drove into the river. They did not survive."
I sighed with disbelief.
"This is serious stuff. They seemed to be so …in control…and well respected. How did they manage to get themselves killed with all the protection they had?"
My mind was racing.
"What about us? They offered us protection. I am very worried about our safety Detective Ferran. Until now we have felt that this whole situation has been a little surreal. It is now getting all too real and I am very concerned

about our well being. Can you give us some protection Detective Ferran?" I asked.
Detective Ferran looked pensive.
"I will do what I can, but you must be honest with me, which I'm sure you will, and you must be brave."
Kay walked over to me and we hugged each other. Not for the first time, we were very scared.

Chapter Eighteen

Reality Check

Cheque de la Realidad

There are many times in life when nothing is as it seems. Life takes a fairly surreal turn and everything seems to be off the mainstream. When this kind of thing happens it is important to remain detached, which is pretty much how you often feel at such a time, and not to panic.

July 31st 2005, 9 a.m - 1o1o, 104 Carrer Sant Miquel, Barceloneta

Detective Ferran was, or so it seemed to us, an excellent detective. He showed no emotion or bias. He didn't force a view or opinion onto you and he listened. He was also very perceptive and asked some very precise and searching questions. He was very economical with his interrogation.

The Detective could see our fear, which was becoming a regular part of our emotional design ever since the events at the Estacion de Franca a couple of days ago. He quickly scanned our faces and he could see that we were not far off panic.

"If what Antich and Alvaro said to you is true, then you must remember that anyone connected with this situation thinks that you are essential to the recovery of the money. No one will hurt you."

He paused. Our faces told him that we were not convinced by his argument.

"Have you any water?" he asked.

"Yes, I'll get you some."

Kay jumped up and entered the kitchen. It was obvious that Ferran was playing games with us. He was trying to calm us down. Kay quickly returned with the water, passed it to the detective and sat down next to me on the sofa. Detective Ferran paused for a while, he was looking at the floor and glanced up at us occasionally. He was clearly thinking carefully about what to say to us. Kay took hold of my hand. The atmosphere in the apartment had taken a turn for the worse. We looked at each other. We were scared and the tension, provided by Detective Ferran's lack of ability to protect us, filled the room. Eventually the detective spoke.

"You must realise that there is a lot of important information in this case. So far seven of the original twelve players in FC Llotja are dead, 5 have died in the last few days. This is a serious situation and one which is taxing the whole of the Mossos d'la Esquadra." He looked away from us and sipped at the water. He looked dreadful.

"I must tell you that we found evidence of recent visitors to the home of Jordi Torras. We do not think that he was alone when he died."

"You think he was murdered?"

My mind was still racing.

"You know that we did not go inside his apartment….the old lady saw us outside."

"You are not suspects….do not worry. However, his death may not be as straightforward as it first seemed." We were both interested by this statement. Why would Ferran be talking to us about this? Surely this is confidential police business? Was he testing out our reaction? By now his conversation had calmed us. Kay was first to compose herself.

"What has any of this got to do with us Detective Ferran? All I am interested in now is our safety."

She stared the detective fully in the eyes. He looked at her then nervously at the floor. He then looked her in the eyes and said.

" You need to know that a computer file we found on his computer gave us a variety of financial information about the Brotherhood and their dealings. We found it in the trash bin. Whoever put it there obviously wanted us to find it or forgot to empty the trash. The file mentioned a security box linked to this apartment that has nothing in it but a piece of paper with a cryptic code. The file also stated that the work of the FC Llotja players resulted in nothing monetary. It was all a hopeful endeavour, but there were no fiscal results."

This was surprising news to us after everything we had been led to believe so far. It was though very reassuring, particularly if it could be proved to be true.

Detective Ferran was in an obvious turmoil. He was very tired, he had had to find out what we knew and yet we knew that he related strongly to us. It was almost possible to see his mind turning over the pro's and con's of giving us more information from his investigations. "What are you thinking Detective?" I asked.

"You seem to be deliberating on our situation."

Slowly, he sipped his glass of water. His fingers ran slowly up and down the outside of the glass as he considered his words.

"OK, vale." He smiled nervously.

"Let's go and check out your security box. That will please me and you. But…we must do it secretly. The problem I have is that I really do not know who to trust in the uniformed Mossos.."

These words were said with determination and energy. He suddenly appeared re-energised, feeding off his spare fuel tank. Despite his questioning of us, Kay and I felt confident and safe with this man.

"Let's go for it," said Kay glancing at me for confirmation. I nodded silently.
"We need to do this quietly and without notice," said the detective.
"Can you get hold of your deeds quickly?"
"Yes." I replied.
"Ever since we have had this apartment there has been many situations when we have needed our documents, either to reconnect our gas supply, pay the electricity bill or apply for a parking permit.
"They are here."
I reached across the table and opened a pink A4 file. The documents that revealed the name of our maintenance company and the deeds with the relevant number on were both in the folder. Ferran smiled.
"Good." He looked up at us.
"I will meet you around the corner on Carrer del Mar. The Mossos outside cannot be trusted. See you in five minutes."
He got up quickly and moved towards the front door to the apartment. Kay made a note of the details we needed. We both got up at the same time and busied ourselves for a few minutes, as we got ready to go.

A few minutes later we were heading down the stairs to the apartment. The officer from the Mossos was day dreaming inside his vehicle as we crept out of the door to the apartment building. It wasn't hard to avoid his gaze, reach the end of the road and turn into Carrer del Mar without him noticing. The familiar faint smell of the sewers hit us as we turned into Carrer del Mar. As we did so we passed one of the many little bars teeming with locals and noise. At this time of the day people were looking for a break from their work, shelter from the sun, a cold beer and a plate of food. There were so many intimate little bars in this area that satisfied these needs.

In front of us was a white Seat Cordoba, its engine humming and with the driver tapping the fingers of his right hand on the top of the steering wheel impatiently and his left arm resting on the door, half sticking out of the window. As we approached the car from behind Detective Ferran turned and beckoned us to hurry. We both climbed into the back seat. The car was a battered specimen of a top of the range model. The leather seats sweated in the heat and the climate control was faulty. "I'm sorry about the condition of the car," muttered Ferran.
"I really don't have time to look after it."
With that Kay and I simultaneously opened our car windows to encourage some through flow of air. The heat of the air coming in was as hot as the air in the car, although the resultant warm draft did help keep our body temperatures in check. Kay had thought ahead and brought a large bottle of water that we took it in turns to drink sips of on a very regular basis. I was wearing a brown muslin shirt and a pair of knee length cotton trousers. These with my open sandals were the coolest and smartest clothes I could find. Kay looked serene in her Quicksilver beach dress. It was pink and white and looked cool. Despite such skimpy apparel we were both sweating heavily within a few minutes of being in the car. Ferran, who had taken his jacket off, had a white shirt and a dark plain blue tie on. He was sweating but not as much as us.
"Hot isn't it?"
He remarked after glancing at us through the rear view mirror.
"It gets better as you get used to it."
The car slowly edged its way through the congested roads of central Barcelona. We were heading straight up through the Eixample area.
"What is the address of the maintenance company?" enquired Ferran.
"Most of them are along Balmes."

Kay took out the deeds of our apartment and scanned them for the address.
"Yes, 365 Carrer de Balmes....you are right Detective Ferran."
It occurred to me that the detective already knew where he was heading. I sensed as we talked in the car that he also knew what we were going to find in the security box. Kay and I were very excited about opening the box, but Ferran was very matter of fact in his attitude.

It took us twenty minutes to get to the address on Balmes. The Seat pulled into a side street and parked on the pavement. We got out and enjoyed the freedom of the air. Our bodies rejoiced from their separation from the hot black leather seats. All three of us stood still, raised our hands in the air and let the cool breeze of the shaded side street envelop our bodies.

Within a few minutes we had moved away from the relative calm and tranquillity of the side street onto the busy thoroughfare that was Carrer de Balmes. The building we were looking for was on the left hand side of the road as we headed on foot away from the city centre. Kay spotted the number 365. The outside of the building was all glass and looked like the entrance to a series of apartments. We went inside and Ferran spoke in Spanish to the attendant who directed us to the lift at the end of the room. The office we were looking for was on the fourth floor. The lift was tatty and dirty and had just enough room for the three of us. As it moved upwards I sensed that we were about to enter a grubby little office of some ancient notary. As the lift clanked to a halt Ferran pushed open the door. It opened immediately into quite a plush room that took Kay and I by surprise. The room was enormous and looked very professional with a large counter, public waiting area and thirty or forty people working at desks and computers in an open plan office environment. There were about ten people either waiting to be attended to or already discussing their business at the counter. Whilst Kay and I hung back, just in front of the lift, stunned by the vista, Ferran immediately arranged with one of the staff some kind of meeting. It was fairly obvious from the speed in which we were dealt with, and by the immediate staff recognition of Ferran, that he had been here before.

The administrator Ferran had spoken to immediately took us up a flight of teak steps. The next floor of the building had a receptionist and several very smart meeting rooms. We were taken into one of these meeting rooms, invited to sit down and offered bottles of water. The room was large with a mahogany rectangular table in the centre of it. Six leather backed chairs with aluminium frames were neatly arranged around the table. Kay and I sat on two of the chairs alongside one of the long sides of the table. Ferran sat at the end of the table nearest the door.
"I will do the talking…ok?" Said Ferran with a forceful air. We just nodded and sat in silence.

Before long a middle-aged man joined us in the room. He had grey, slicked back hair, thick dark rimmed glasses and a small grey/black moustache. In his black suit he looked much older than he probably was. It was quite chilly in the room, which was heavily air-conditioned. The man sat down and welcomed us. His name was Alfredo Jimenez. He looked at us and spoke very quickly in Spanish. We had no idea what he said. Ferran interpreted.
"Senor Jimenez welcomes you and says he knows this is a very serious situation. If you show him the deeds to the maintenance of you apartment and your identification, passports would be good, then you can see your security box."

Kay handed all the documents over to the administrator. We were very tense. The office was very formal and this, after all, could provide the explanation to the origins of all our difficulties of the past two days.

Senor Jimenez looked over the documents Kay had given him. He quickly looked up and signalled to a young lady who was standing near the doorway to the room we were in. The young lady was in her late twenties and had a lovely light brown skin and jet-black long hair tied up neatly. She wore all white: A lace T-shirt and a white flowing dress. The heels she wore showed off her very shapely legs. She strolled over to the table carrying a large rectangular metal case. When she reached the table she gently put down on the table in front of Senor Jimenez. He spoke again this time with gestures.
"He is showing you that the code on the security box matches the code on the deeds to your apartment." Observed Ferran. I leant forward and checked that the two sets of numbers did match. I nodded in agreement towards Senor Jimenez. He took a key out of his pocket and opened the lock on the security box. He then pushed the box across the table in front of Kay and I. We looked at each other and then at Ferran.
"Go on then open it," he instructed.
Kay lifted up the two metal latches and opened the case. Inside the case was a purple felt lining. Lying in the centre of the case were two small envelopes. She reached in and pulled them out. Kay placed the two envelopes on the table in front of us. Neither was sealed and we could see from the colour of the paper and the ink on them that they were both fairly old. Kay looked up at Ferran. He understood. He asked Senor Jimeniz and his attendant to leave the room. They realised that we wanted to be alone and left the room hurriedly and apologetically, closing the door behind them. Ferran got out of his chair and stood

behind us to get a better view. Kay pulled a piece of paper out of the first envelope that was marked with a single word: 'Losiento'.

The paper was folded over four times. Kay unfurled it. We all looked at the writing. Kay and I understood most of it but Ferran was left to fully decipher it for us.
"What it says is this:

Dear comrades, we had such a good time together as FC La Llotja. We were a real team and we forged some very special bonds. I will remember those days very well and with joy for the rest of my life. However, we made some very dangerous plans at the end of our union and most of us worked hard to make them happen. The problem was that each of us had different motives for our combined action. Most of us wanted financial security, although some wanted further power and were keen to use our gains for political ends.

Our efforts netted many million pesetas, not much of this could be given directly to each of us as it is all tied up in property developments. The route to this money though, as you can see, is not here. Also, I must inform you, that in the early 1980's, I was instructed by one member of our team, to release a large proportion of our amassed funds to purchase particular properties in the area just along the coast from our beloved Barceloneta. The area that is proposed as the Olympic Village, if our city's bid is successful. The reason for this action was simply, I was told, to further the political ends of Catalonia. I did not agree that he should be allowed to do this but in the circumstances, which I shall not go into now, I had no alternative. I was aware through my association with Santiago Lines of the location and code number of the security box. Unfortunately others also knew that I had this information. By the time you read this it will not be important, as I am sure that the financial wealth of the Brotherhood will have been put to use in furthering the career of an individual in the name of Catalonia and it will be too late to do anything about it.

As you can probably tell, I have been allowed to write this as an apology to all the members of FC La Llotja. It is very unlikely that anyone will ever read this but just in case you do, I can not mention the name of the person who instructed me to utilise the funds of FC La Llotja in the name of Catalonia.

I am so very sorry for betraying your trust.

The letter was signed: Albert Cots.

We were both a little surprised. Albert Cots had died several years ago shortly after relocating the finances of the Brotherhood.
"You knew about this already didn't you," I accused Ferran.
"Read the second note first, then I will explain," he replied.

Kay looked at the second envelope. There was no writing on the outside of it. She took the paper out. There were only a few words on it. We could both read them clearly:

"Stop Julian Solbes and the Popular Front of Catalonia!"

Chapter Nineteen

Dazed and confused

Deslumbrado y confundido

Sometimes life is very confusing, things that happen in life just don't make sense. The brain feels under pressure and bombarded by information that leaves you feeling dazed. The feeling is out of the ordinary and can be debilitating.

July 31st 2005, 11 a.m – Carrer Balmes, Barcelona

"Information from the file we found at the home of Jordi Torras told us what to expect from the security box. The exact words were mentioned in the file. I came up yesterday to confirm the findings as I had a warrant to open up the security box." revealed an apologetic Detective Ferran.
"I really don't care whether you have been here or not," I said.
"What worries me is the fact that all this is probably a hoax. None of us, now that Antich and Alvaro are dead, have any idea of the truth. Is there any real wealth in the Brotherhood or has it all been diverted?"
'Can't you just arrest Solbes," asked Kay with a very frustrated sigh.
"We believe that there is still a great deal of money linked to the Brotherhood. And although we are beginning to collect quite a lot of evidence against Solbes, there is nowhere near enough yet to really convict him. Not that the judiciary in Barcelona would!" observed Ferran.
"How can you say that: Isn't this proof?" asked Kay holding up the paper from the second envelope.

"You may think so," said the detective, "….but, there is no real evidence: Simply a note in a security box. We don't know who wrote it. It could have been me. All this could be a set up."
"That's not good enough." I replied.
"Our lives are obviously now at risk. We want some help. Solbes is a powerful man and is obviously involved in some way. Why can't you take some kind of action?"
Ferran looked at the floor, he then slowly looked up at Kay then me.
"You have no idea of just who you are dealing with. Julian Solbes is an extremely clever man. He is a supreme politician. Everything he does is political. He says 'hello' and it is political. He knows people and he works people. It is hard to identify people who are not in his influence. Solbes is Senor Catalonia. Even people who hate the man as a person like his championing of the nation."
Ferran paused.
"I loathe the man. But I know of few others who feel the same way as me. Also, I do not agree with you about your safety. Whoever is behind all this has an excellent information source. They will know that we have been here and they will know that there is nothing in the box. You will be of no use to them."

I was astonished by Ferran's view of Solbes.
"My heart really bleeds for the state of Catalonia if what you say is true. What we see is a corrupt and egotistical politician trying for personal gain to influence the situation in this region. Surely we need to do something if we are to change the history and future of this region. I might be new to this wonderful region and already I love Catalonia, but it has to be honest and fair."

Detective Ferran was in some kind of turmoil. He was half English and half Catalan. He loved Catalonia but his

genes exercised the English sense of fair play. He paused. He looked at Kay and then at me.
“I really like you two. I feel that we are one, a team. You are both English but you love Barcelona. I am a mixture of Catalan and English. We are very similar.’
Kay, who had been lost in deep thought and concentration for a while, suddenly came alive.
“OK then, help us. Like you, we want to know what is going on. We would love you to solve the mysteries of all the murders, but we really want our lives back. We also want Catalonia to succeed, so what do we do?” she said.
Ferran looked at me. His face was totally expressionless. He burst out laughing.
“What does it matter?” He said. “Life is about more than this.”
I had to agree. Although we did want to know what were we involved in and why?
“Why are you a policeman if that is what you believe?” I asked.
“It is a very long story but it is because I share some of your views that I am a policeman that wants to create a society that is fair and just. Unfortunately a lot of people who have influence over my work do not feel the same.”
“You must have come across a lot of frustrations.” interjected Kay.
“You come to accept it. You also find, like in any job, the people you want to work with who you can trust and whose company you enjoy.” mused Ferran.
“I have a few good people who I work with and who I can trust, but there is no one senior to me who I feel this way about.”
Ferran looked up at us and then at the floor. It was if he realised he was opening up to us too much and revealing his inner thoughts.
“It is dangerous this kind of talk. It makes you discontented....and, despite the frustrations and the

corruption I still love my job and I know that I make a difference to this society we live in. Barcelona is a very tolerant place. The people tolerate each other and that makes for a generally accepting and peaceful society. As a result I tolerate an element of corruption and inefficiency. I don't like it, but I work around it."

He stood up proudly.

"And now I must go. Thank you for your company and for your openness. I will keep you informed of the outcome of our investigations, but I think for everyone's interests that you two must now stay out of this situation. I cannot believe that anyone will want to bother you now. I will let it be known that there was nothing in the security box and word will soon spread that you two are unimportant. However, we will keep a guard on you for a couple of days."

With that statement he smiled and walked out of the room. Kay and I looked at each other and sighed. From both of us, it was a sigh of relief.

We followed Ferran out of the room and caught up with him waiting for the lift. He was smiling.

"This case is getting very involved. There is much more to it than you could ever imagine I don't want you two involved anymore in doing your own thing…you know…investigating the names on the list. But you can keep your eyes open. Let me know if you see any of the people you have seen so far."

We stepped into the lift and Kay pressed the button for the ground floor.

"Ok, but you will keep us informed won't you?' asked Kay.

I joined in.

"Yes, we really don't want anymore danger but we feel we could be of use to you."

Ferran said nothing. He stepped first out of the lift. As we walked towards the entrance of the building he offered us a ride back to Barceloneta.
"You have been very useful and I have a feeling that you will have more to do in this investigation. Do you need a ride?"
Kay and I sensed our mutual need for a little space and thinking time.
"Thank you, but I think we will stroll back under our own steam. You obviously have a lot of work to do and could probably do without the detour to Barceloneta." I suggested.
"True on all counts. Ok, see you soon. Take care and don't talk to any strange men!" he laughed.
"I will make sure that your apartment is watched over the next couple of days. In public though stay amongst the crowds!"
He flashed us another wicked smile as he pushed open the double glass door and disappeared down Carrer de Balmes.

The air hit us like opening an oven door as we stepped out from the air-conditioned building into the street. It was around midday now, although it felt much, much later.
"I like Ferran," observed Kay. "I trust him."
I had to agree. We could sense that he liked us and trusted us.
"Let's get some breakfast," I suggested. "I could die for a coffee."
"Don't speak like that" said Kay, hitting me in the stomach. "Especially with everything that is going on."
I put my arm around her and guided her down along Balmes. We both put our heads back and soaked up the sun that was streaming across the city.

Chapter Twenty

Free and easy

Libre y fácil

Sometimes you look forward to a break or a holiday so much that when it comes it is a disappointment. Holidays in particular can be very stressful and sometimes not very relaxing. The best and perhaps most relaxing times are often immediately after a stressful and busy experience, before you have had time to gather your thoughts or to make plans on how to enjoy your relaxation time. If you can relax, avoid planning, hang loose and stay free and easy, then you will have a good chance of total relaxation.

July 31st 2005, 1 p.m – Central Barcelona

An hour later we had been refuelled by a couple of café con leches and a cana de crema each. The sun was still filling the sky and the city sweltered. We cut across the square in front of the Cathedral. The grand building was still being externally refurbished and had huge areas of its frontage covered by scaffolding and posters. We had yet to see the building in its full glory, as the renovation work obviously was extensive and lengthy. This was not one of our favourite areas of the city. Full of tourists and consequently, beggars. If you wanted to lose your camera or purse this was the place to come, certainly in the tourist season. It had always amazed Kay and I, how arrogant North-Western European and American tourists could be. Not only were they incredibly loud and intent on only speaking their own language, but they also dressed openly as tourists. I am sure that these people don't wear checked shorts and funny little hats when they are at home but in the sun it seems to become the tourist costume. Such clothes when accompanied by the regular tourist accessories of bum bag, camera and tourist map are the equivalent to someone wearing a big sign on their head saying, 'I am a tourist – rip me off'.

Kay and I hurried through the square carefully avoiding the tourist hordes. We needed some water so we cut across Via Laeitana and headed into the newly rebuilt market of Santa Catarina. It was relatively cool inside the market hall. The high roof of the building at least provided a shield from the hot penetrating afternoon sun. The market was in the middle of its typical mid-afternoon lull. It was either lunch or siesta time, or even just simply too hot for people to spend their time haggling after vegetables, meat and fish. The fish on display in these city markets was always fascinating because of its variety. The size, colour, and general appearance made people want to touch and experiment. I held Kay's hand as we sauntered through the relaxed market atmosphere. We casually looked at the displays before placing a few cents into the hand of a stallholder in return for a chilled two-litre bottle of water. Soon we reached the far side of the market and found ourselves on Carrer Colomines. We paused and took it in turns to take a few gulps each of the cool water. It was a very hot day. Even in the cool streets that were protected from the sun by the height of the buildings, it was still stifling.
"There are still a few hours of good sun left," suggested Kay.
"Let's take our time getting back to the apartment, grab some lunch by the waterside and the have a couple of relaxed hours on the beach."
"What do you think?"
I really wasn't thinking much at all. My brain had gone into one of those periods common to us all. It had almost totally shutdown. The last couple of months had been very

busy at work and I had been really looking forward to switching off on holiday when all this happened. With Ferran convinced that the Brotherhood affair was mostly sorted and out of our hands, I had just gone into a complete relaxed mode, physically and mentally. I was just glugging on the bottle of water and looking totally vacant.

Kay had sauntered mischievously back over to a fish stall, just inside the market, and picked up a huge flat fish that looked like a stingray. “Charlie. Charlie. What do you think? Fancy something exotic for tea?”

“Ugh, ohh. I really don’t mind. I really don’t want to make any decisions.”

Kay placed the fish down with some disappointment and jogged to catch up with me. We moved off down the street before cutting down through the alley that led to Caller Corders. There were an increasing number of people about. Tourists were taking in the atmosphere and locals were going about their business. The smell of fried cooking pleasantly wafted around us as we strolled down the alley. The numerous little bars and café’s along the street were serving up a variety of tapas. This area of the barrio was undergoing a good deal of redevelopment and reconstruction and so the little bars were full of construction workers eating, drinking and discussing the intricacies of daily life in this city.

It would have been an embarrassing understatement to describe our present behaviour as anything other than that normally associated with a couple of young lovers. We were slowly relaxing into each other again as we strolled arm in arm along the street, reliving the first day or so of our holiday. Every now and then we stopped to kiss. Then we would slowly head off again towards an unknown and irrelevant destination. We were both slipping into relaxed holiday mode.

"I think it's beer time," said Kay slipping her hand under my shirt and stroking my lower back as we walked.
"Are we far from the park?"
Kay's sense of direction and awareness of place had improved remarkably recently but she was still a little unsure of how places fitted together in her mental image of the city.
"Parc Estacio du Nord? The one opposite that new apartment we fancied last year?"
Last year we had found a newly renovated apartment block that housed what appeared to be our dream apartment. The only trouble was the price. Instead we settled for our much smaller apartment and an occasional visit to the park opposite the dream apartment.
"Yes. That's the one," smiled the woman I loved immensely.

"If we head along here….. it's a little out of the way but we will be there in 10 minutes." I replied.
Our pace quickened slightly now that we had a renewed sense of purpose and a clear destination. Water in this heat was essential, although it was a poor substitute for sipping a cold beer whilst sitting in the glorious sun.

The black iron gates of the Parc de Estacio du Nord were wide open and the sandy gravel walkways stretched out invitingly to the casual visitor. The park was small; it was the size of several football pitches. The park had a unique visual character. The left hand side of the park was rimmed by the Estacio du Nord; it was now a bus station and it provided quite a grand backdrop. All the other edges of the park were fringed by high-rise apartment buildings, five or six storeys high. These apartments were all either newly renovated or totally new, this was an attractive area to live. There was not much to the park. Central and circular, wide walkways flanked grassy mounds fronted by bizarre, but beguiling, ceramic mosaics on a grand scale. The mosaics glinted in the high afternoon sun as Kay and I sauntered along the central walkway. We were heading for a brown hut like building in the centre of the park. This building served coffee, beer and snacks and was surrounded by twenty or so chairs, open to the sun. The seats were a welcome sight. We were by now very thirsty. The water bottle was empty and long gone. Kay slumped in one of the metal chairs. I took the few extra steps to the opening in the little hut. The girl behind the bar was about 19 years old and she looked Andulucian. Very dark hair and slightly less sophisticated than the natural Catalans. "Dos cervezas y uno bottella de agua sin gas."

Sitting in the park, sipping beer, feeling the cool breeze that had tripped the mile or so from the sea. Kay and I sat back and relaxed.

Chapter Twenty-One

On the trail

En el rastro

Detective movies are always quite exciting, particularly when they involve some kind of chase. Most people never get that level of excitement, that's why action films do good business at the box office. The closest some of us come to a chase is when we sometimes have to follow somebody. It may be your partner or a friend or even when you suspect a total stranger of doing something illegal. Following someone, prying into their activities and conversations, whilst staying out of sight, is both harmless and exciting. The trick is not to be seen or caught.

July 31st 2005, 1.30 p.m – Parc Estacion du Nord, Barcelona

A young woman in her thirties was struggling with a baby in a sling, clinging to the front of her body, whilst at the same time trying to control a three year old who was intent on tormenting a terrier like dog of a passer by. "No, Paula, come here. That is not the way to behave."
The woman was extremely well dressed, in casual long cream linen shorts and a matching linen shirt. Her hair was jet black with well-coiffured gold streaks. Her thick black-rimmed shades gave her an exotic and expensive look. This was confirmed by the delicate nature of the very expensive light tan sandals she was wearing. She was struggling to control the three year old girl. Eventually she slumped down at a table next to us. As she relaxed into the chair, with the baby fast asleep nestling in her chest, she let out an exhausted sigh. The three year old

temporarily climbed into one of the aluminium chairs then jumped out and crawled under the matching metal table, looking to be grateful of the shade it provided. Kay was watching the action and reacted quickly.

"Puedo ayudarle?"

"Si, gracias." Replied the relieved woman.

"Puedo tener una cervesa y una zumo de naranja para mi hija?"

The woman provided a 10 euro note out of nowhere and placed it in Kay's hand. Kay smiled and went over to the hatch in the service hut and ordered the drinks. Kay looked back at the woman and her children and smiled. Kay had always rejected the idea of having children ever since she had met me. Managing two totally new teenagers, Susie and Joe, my children from a previous marriage, had made her realise how hard a job it was. However, often she saw little children and appeared all misty eyed. She soon snapped out of it though on this occasion as the little girl broke free of her seated mother and ran towards the gate of the park and a busy road.

"Paula!"

Her mother screamed. Kay took off and secured the little girl by her hand and led her, amazingly quietly, back to her mother.

"Oh, muchas gracias, muchas gracias," said the woman before chastising the girl who had by now plonked herself down on a seat giving Kay an icy but respectful stare. Kay eventually carried over the drinks to the mini-family and slumped back in her chair next to me.

"Kids! No thanks."

She took a huge gulp of her beer and rested her arms on the side of the chair as she sunk her neck backwards to rest on my shoulder. She spent a few seconds staring at the pure blue sky.

The weather was exceptionally warm. The sky was clear and there was no wind at all. I sweated sitting still. The brown linen shirt and matching three quarter length linen trousers I was wearing, both revealed patches of wetness from my leaking pores. I drank more to keep cool. Instead of reducing my temperature, the liquid appeared to simply refuel my leaking pores. The park was ideal for this kind of afternoon: peaceful and very visual. The ceramic sculptures gave the park a fairly surreal feature and provided a constantly interesting vista. I finished off my beer.

"Another?" I quizzed Kay.

She didn't have to answer. I knew. As I got up to order a couple more beers the lady and her two children got up to leave.

"Adios," she waved to Kay, in particular, and they quickly moved off towards the park entrance on Carrer Almongavers. We watched them go. The mother, who was very attractive, struggling with her baby and young daughter. I turned back towards Kay smiling. Our eyes met and we enjoyed a few moments of mutual appreciation. Then, just behind Kay, but in the near distance, I caught sight of a figure shuffling awkwardly along the park pathway. Coming towards us, but heading towards the same park exit just taken by the women and the children, was a very distracted young man. It was Jordi Badia, the same man who had accosted me at the station and then demanded the list of names from us a day or so ago. He was well dressed in a dark grey suit, white shirt and blue patterned tie. He didn't look hot. His neat beard was out of place with his now dishevelled dark hair. As he walked he was constantly looking behind himself as if he was being followed. Kay followed my glance and saw him approach us. We watched him in silence. He passed within a couple of yards of us but he was so distracted he didn't notice us. It was clear to see that he was in some distress. His face was red around the eyes and it was obviously not from the heat as there were no signs of sweat on his face or his clothes. He did appear to be crying though. As he drifted passed us on the path we could hear his faint sobbing. Within a few seconds he had reached the park exit. He stopped, looked to his left and then right and finally back the way he had come before lurching off to the right and across the road.

Kay looked at me.
"What was that all about? We must follow him. Something is going on with that guy."
"Ok. I think your right but I think it is a mistake to follow him. We are just getting out of this mess and you want to get back into it." I said in frustration.
"No I don't but he may lead us to someone or something interesting that can help Ferran."
"Alright, but we must keep out of sight. He must not see us following him."
Kay acknowledged me with a nod and leapt out of her seat. It took me a second or two to gulp down as much of the beer I had just bought as I could before taking a few long steps to catch Kay as she headed for the park exit.

By the time we got to the wrought tall iron gates at the exit to the park we could see no sign of Jordi Badia. From my standing position near the serving hatch of the shack in the park though, I had managed to see the rough direction he had headed. We gambled and ran over the carriageway and down the 100 metres of road towards the next intersection. There, a further 100 metres away, was Jordi Badia. He seemed to have calmed down a little but he was still fairly agitated. He appeared to be heading towards the Ciuatedella Park, which was only a few blocks away from where we were. I grabbed Kay's hand and move us in line with the trees that followed, uniformly, the road at twenty metres gaps. Even if he turned round, which he continued to do, he would not be able to see us. We ran between the trees, gradually getting closer to him. By now I was a sea of sweat. Rivers of liquid ran across all parts of my body either soaking my clothes or dripping from the end of my nose. Kay was an ice maiden in comparison.

At the next crossing the lights changed just as we got to them. We decided to cross over and try to get ahead of Jordi Badia as he went through the Ciutadella Parc. As we crossed the road, amidst a flurry of Chinese tourists, we were trying to keep one eye on our target and one eye on avoiding each of the tourists, who, like most tourists intent on enjoying the experiences and sights of a new city, had no awareness of personal space or of what was around them. We went straight across the road and into an entrance to the park. At the same moment that we went through the park gates so did Jordi Badia, albeit through a different entrance some 75 metres further along the road.

Parc de Ciutadella is a beautiful park. It lies on the site of the old Citadel that had apparently governed the city a couple of hundred years ago. At that time the place was one of hatred, whereas today the park was a place of relaxation and joy. The large park is also the home of the Catalan Parliament buildings. The centrepiece of the whole park is a huge Gaudi designed statuesque water fountain that had recently been cleaned up and was working again after years of neglect and overgrowth. We passed behind the fountain anticipating that Jordi would take one of the long pathways that ran parallel to each other down the centre of the park. Kay and I jogged along eventually passing the central lake under the shade of a variety of leafy trees.

Kay held out her hand in front of my waist. I stopped suddenly.
"Where is he? I can't see him."
"That's him there." I said as I pointed to a figure coming towards us on the other side of the lake.
"No. That's not him."
Kay's eyesight was not the best but on this occasion I could see now that she was right.
"Come on. He must have cut across out of the park early onto Passeig de Picasso."
I grabbed her hand and we sprinted towards he nearest park exit. As we did so we nearly ran into Jordi Badia. We were lucky as the park was very busy at this time of day, with tourists enjoying the green break from the concrete of the city and workers making the most of shade afforded by the park trees during their siesta break. There were several other people that were part of a crowd walking in the same direction as Jordi. Kay and I kept walking diagonally away from where he was heading. He hadn't seen us. He was much calmer now. He was no longer distractedly looking all about him, but instead he was focused on the ground in front of him as he walked. It was clear that he was running a number of things intensely through his mind.

Several minutes later we had managed to keep pace with Jordi Badia as he entered an apartment building back on Carrer Balboa in Barceloneta. Directly opposite was the Café Ca La Montse. Kay and I decided to sit and watch for a while. Inside the café there was an excellent air conditioning system in operation that instantly leapt to work on my body temperature. As Kay ordered a couple of café americanos I went into the toilets to try to rescue my appearance and dry off a little. Kay sat at a table at the window. The café was part of a restaurant and was quite chic in its décor, lots of redwood panels and quality

furniture. There were only a couple of other people in the café. It wasn't long before I joined Kay at the window table.
"Anything? Thanks for the coffee."
"No, but it's nice to sit down!" Kay smiled.
"He could be in there for ages. He did look very upset though."
"He did. There is much more to this than we know."
I replied before taking a careful sip of the piping hot coffee.

Ten minutes passed. Then two apparently unconnected things happened simultaneously. The same lady we had seen in the park earlier, struggling with the two children, came into the café alone, ordered a café cortado and sat down at the far side of the room. She hadn't seen me and Kay but as she sat down she looked relieved to be without her two charges. At the same time, in the road outside, a white transit van pulled up suddenly after partly mounting the pavement. All four doors of the van opened, the drivers, the passengers and the two doors at the rear. Out of each door came a heavily built man. Each one looked grim and dangerous. They each wore a focussed and determined expression and each of them carried a wrench or a baseball bat. The group of men went towards the door that led to the apartment block that Jordi Badia had entered several minutes ago. The elder of the four men had very short cropped black hair and a reddish/brown face. He led the way and put his foot against the lock mechanism of the door to the apartment block, he took the step almost in his normal stride. The door flew open with a loud crash. Everyone in the street and in the café stopped and looked at the source of the crash. The men hurried into the apartment block.

The lady who we had seen in the park was now standing watching from the rear of the café. She had picked up her mobile and was frantically speaking to someone. She closed her blue Razr phone, put it in her jacket pocket, which looked like a Zara classic, and moved towards the café entrance. As she moved she reached inside her jacket and took hold of a small gun that she had obviously had in a shoulder holster. Kay and I watched this action with our mouths open. Our eyes followed the glamorous woman with a gun in her hand as she raced outside the cafe and across the street towards the source of the action. As she disappeared into the apartment building, following the four men, a beat up white Seat Cordoba raced into the street followed by a Mossos d'Esquadra car. Both cars hit the brakes hard as they reached the café. Detective Ferran, with an assistant, probably another detective raced out of their car, closely followed by two Mossos squad men. All four ran into the apartment building. There was a lot of shouting coming from the upper floors of the apartment building. On the third floor balcony of the building one of the men that had gone into the apartment appeared. He seemed to take a look at his options for escape before deciding to go back into the apartment. At that point a shot rang out and the shouting stopped.

After a few minutes a Mossos officer appeared dragging behind him one of the men by a pair of handcuffs. He had his hands in front of him and he looked a little shocked. Two of the other men followed both in handcuffs and each accompanied by one of the policemen. The older man, who had kicked open the door then appeared. He had his right hand handcuffed to Detective Ferran, and his left arm hung limply by his side. There was blood on his blue long sleeved shirt, but not much. It looked like a surface wound. All these men were put into one of the two cars and watched over by the police officers or detectives.

Finally Jordi Badia came out of the apartment building. He wasn't in handcuffs but he looked a real mess. His nose was smashed against his face and there was blood all over his head. It ran down his neck and most of the length of his shirt. Despite this he was quite composed and was gesticulating with his hands to the woman who had been in the café minutes earlier, as she guided him into the Seat by his arm. Within minutes the whole show was over. The cars had raced off and everyone went back to their normal business. Kay and I looked at each other questioningly.
"We need to get in touch with Detective Ferran to find out exactly what is going on," I said.

Chapter Twenty-Two

The Truth

La Verdad

People spend their whole lives searching for the truth. The vast majority of lives are a lie, with people not accepting who they are or acknowledging the pointlessness of their lives. The truth about oneself arrives when you fully understand who you are, take responsibility for your actions, and don't blame others for your mistakes. Also, when you realise that you are totally unique, and whatever you bring to life, no one else can match it. The truth about other people is harder to come by.

July 31st 2005, 8 p.m – Café Colombo, Barceloneta

We didn't feel like eating. We had enjoyed the tracking of Jordi Badia, although the sequence of events that followed this activity had disturbed us. Neither of us felt good about ourselves. We felt a little responsible for the beating of Jordi Badia. Even though it had been nothing to do with us, we felt that we may have led the four thugs to his doorstep. Had we? Who was the woman in the café? How had Ferran and the police got to the situation so quickly? What happened in the apartment block? These and other questions hung heavily in our heads and formed the basis of our conversation over a few beers in the Café Colombo. We were sat just inside the entrance to the bar on our favourite couple of stools alongside the bar itself.

It wasn't long before we had some kind of answer to our questions. The mysterious glamorous woman who had haunted us with her presence in the park earlier in the day sat at the bar on the stool to my left. I was quite shocked to see her sitting there, although I was surprised that anyone had chosen to sit there at all, considering the bar was nearly empty, full of vacant chairs and tables. I half glanced to my left, almost immediately I had to take another look. She was particularly attractive. Close up I could see she was in her mid-thirties, although the lines around her eyes told many stories. She wore heavy but well applied make-up and you could tell it wasn't to cover up blemishes, but to add to her attraction. However, she looked tired.

"Hola," she said as if we had been friends for years.

At that moment Detective Ferran sat himself alongside Kay on another stool. Kay looked equally surprised.

"The very least you two could do is buy us both a beer."

"What do you mean?" I queried back to Ferran. At the same time though I attracted the bar mans attention and signalled for four new beers.

"You have got us involved in a very complex case. I for one am exhausted."

"We've got you involved." said Kay indignantly.

"Yes, you have." Ferran was smiling. "Really though, I have to say, this case is fascinating."

We looked at him. His colleague shuffled, vying some of the attention that she was obviously used to receiving.

"Let me introduce you to Detective Maria Fernandez Tupelo. I think you may have run into her earlier today." I turned and smiled at her. Kay was warm but could see my obvious attraction to her and immediately suggested we moved to a table across the other side of the bar room where we could sit and face each other. We moved with our beers.

Maria spoke reasonably good English but was generally very content to listen. Ferran told us how Maria had been watching us for the past twenty four hours and ran into us in the park, when her 'disguise' involving looking after her sisters two children got a little out of hand. She had managed to drop them off at her sisters apartment near the park and caught up with us in the café later. She too had seen Jordi Badia and had telephoned Ferran at regular intervals to tell him their location. Kay and I couldn't understand the involvement with Jordi Badia at this stage.

"What had he done?" she asked.

Detective Fernandez Tupelo started to answer but decided that her English wasn't quite up to it. Ferran, looking livelier by each swig of beer, leapt gallantly to her vocal support.

"Earlier today one of our superiors told me he had been given a lead that Jordi Badia was plotting to discredit Julian Solbes with some kind of misinformation scandal. He wouldn't tell me where his lead came from but he also added that Badia had leaked false information to the TV companies and the press about the deaths of his father, Xavier Badia, Jose Baquero and Rafael Gastesi."

"You're joking?" I gasped.

"No, not at all. So Jefe Inspector Domingez told us to pick Jordi Badia up for questioning. We were on the way when Detective Fernandez Tupelo phoned in with her information."

As he spoke he intimated towards the female detective with his eyes. Like Ferran, each sip of beer was making her look more and more relaxed. She was beginning to glow and her sultry attractiveness was becoming increasingly evident. Her relationship and attitude towards Ferran made it obvious that they had, probably in the not too distant past, been casual lovers. In her eyes was a knowing interest in him. Although they also revealed a desire to explore him further. Ferran for his part treated her with a respect he didn't readily offer anyone else. He looked at her with a longing that said I've been there, I liked it and I want more. It was interesting reading these unspoken signs although it was pretty obvious that there was a distance between them that said that there was nothing happening at the moment.

"Have you spoken to Jordi Badia then?" questioned Kay looking at Ferran and getting an affirmative reply through a combination of his eyes and eyebrow movement as he sipped his beer.
"What did he have to say? I find it hard to believe he set up his father's death. When we saw him after the incident at Estacion de Franca he actually said that he didn't think his father was dead."
"It was very interesting when we spoke to him. I think he realised that we had just saved him from a nasty beating. Those four thugs had obviously been sent by the same source that had tipped us of. Someone wanted to teach him a lesson to get him to keep his mouth shut."
"Why?" I said, "Was he really going to set up Solbes. I thought he worked for him?"
"Well. This is where it gets really interesting. Badia didn't tell us everything but he was up to something. He believed that the list of names he got off you two held the key to whatever he was up to. Apparently his father had told him about the Brotherhood and their money one night when they got drunk together. Jordi Badia said that his father had said that the Brotherhood had made so much money but it was impossible for anyone to track it, but that the paper with the names on was the key."
"So that's why he was so desperate to get it." asked Kay.
"Si, pero he need not the money," interjected Detective Fernandez Tupelo, desperate to get in on the conversation.
"Yeah," continued Ferran.
"He had another reason to try to get at Solbes. He obviously thought he could find out some more scandal about the Brotherhood to get at Solbes."
"How could he work for someone he obviously hated?" said Kay with a very puzzled look on her face. By now

the bar was beginning to fill up both locals and tourists. The noise level in the bar had increased significantly and we needed more beers. I quickly nipped across to the bar.
"Don't tell us anymore until I get back." I instructed as I left our little cabal.

What I really love about Spain was evident in this bar now. It was a plain bar with a big three sided counter with tapas, beer, wine and coffee available. Newspapers and magazines were plentiful and people came into the bar to socialise or to just chill out, read and relax. No one hurried them along and no one was in a hurry. It was now getting on for 10 p.m and after several beers I felt very mellow. I looked across at Kay. She was glowing from the sun and from the atmosphere. She looked beautiful especially when she laughed. She was enjoying the company of Ferran and Detective Fernandez Tupelo. They looked like three friends out for a drink. That's what I liked about Ferran. He looked anything but a policeman. His colleague looked even less like one.

I sat back down and joined in the on-going conversation. Kay grabbed my arm teasingly and spoke to the two detectives.
"Go on you two tell Charlie what you just said, he'll love it."
"What's going on?" I said with a smile.
They all laughed.
Detective Fernandez Tupelo replied first with a shy smile on her face.
"I asked Kay how old you two were, as I thought you were an ideal couple."
"Meaning," said Kay " that we were about the same age!"
"I thought you were both late thirties," added Ferran in a manner that left me guessing as to whether or not he really believed that.

"I was very surprised when Kay told me how old you really were!"
They all laughed.

Eventually we got back to the interview with Jordi Badia. Ferran continued with the details.
"The most fascinating thing is this."
He looked around him furtively and spoke quietly. We all leaned towards him to listen to what he had to say. "You must not tell anyone else this. I am not being at all professional here but I am telling you because you have helped and will continue to help with this investigation."
The tension was building. Ferran paused to gather his words.

"Jordia Badia was not Xavier Badia's son."
"What," we all gasped, including Detective Fernandez Tupelo. This was obviously the first she had heard of this. We looked at Ferran astonished, begging him with our eyes to tell us more.
"He really opened up about this. The four thugs had just had time to smash his nose when we got there and so he was feeling pretty sore. It was obvious that someone to do with Solbes was behind the beating, but Badia also made it obvious that the beating had scared him off and he wasn't going to pursue anything to do with Solbes. I think he had been a little naive in his actions and very idealistic about what it would achieve."
Kay looked distracted as if she had just thought of something, she had.
"Did we hear a gunshot this afternoon?"
"Yes," answered Ferran.
"Detective Fernandez Tupelo warned one of the guys to stop hitting Badia but he didn't, so she winged him in the arm."

As he spoke he looked admiringly at the female detective who at this moment looked more like a high class TV presenter than a gun wielding defender of liberty.
"Tell us more about Badia" I urged.
"Well," paused Ferran.
"Apparently, Xavier Badia told Jordi during this same drunken conversation I mentioned before, which by the way only occurred a couple of weeks ago, that he wasn't his son. He said that he loved Julian Solbes and that he would do anything for him. Apparently he had a deep physical attraction to Solbes which was unrequited, but these feelings still made him incredibly loyal to the man."
"I really don't understand," said Kay for us all.
"Well, this is the interesting bit. Twenty-five or so years ago, Julian Solbes got a girl pregnant. He was married and the girl came from a wealthy banking family. It would have ruined Solbes' marriage, his fledgling political career and his life, had it got out. In Spain at that time it was just not acceptable to have an affair or to get divorced, let alone to have an illegitimate child."
"So what happened?" I asked.
"Xavier Badia agreed to marry the girl and pass off Jordi as his own son."
We all sat back into our chairs and looked at each other in amazement. It was hard to fathom that the tale we had just been told was true.
"I know it sounds incredible but Jordi Badia told us all this on oath and it is recorded. It will not go any further as he does not want it to and he does not want a blood test. He said he had no idea until a few weeks ago that the person he was working for was his real father."
"You can see why he was in real turmoil," said Kay sympathetically.
"Amazing. Absolutely amazing." I reflected.

Chapter Twenty-three

Angels

Ángeles

Angels play a large part in all our lives. Most people are touched by an angel, often without even knowing it. Angels bring us love, hope and well-being. Angels are rare, but when you meet one you know it. As in the words of Nick Cave: "I don't believe in the existence of angels, but looking at you I wonder if that's true."

July 31st 2005, 12 midnight – Café Colombo, Barceloneta

We had had too much to drink to meet any angels tonight. After Ferran had told us the Jordi Badia story, the four of us had continued to forge the beginnings of what could develop into an excellent friendship. Detective Fernandez Tupelo was now known as Maria to us all and she had proved to be really down to earth and very amusing. Kay and I had done our best to cement the lingering, smouldering relationship between the two detectives and it was obvious where they would both be spending the night. As we left Bar Colombo to a rousing, "Adios' from the moustached barman, we paused outside on the cobbles. The night was magnificent. The air was still and there was little nearby traffic. The lights of the marina in front of us glistened on the harbour water of the Port Vell. The air smelt both fresh and dirty at the same time. The night breezes had only just started to filter out the stagnant aroma of the blistering day. Ferran and Maria, and Kay and I were arm in arm. The two detectives headed off towards the beach as we started over the road.

"Tomorrow at 10 a.m. Pan I Mes Café. I have a job for you two. Hasta la vista!" shouted Ferran as they stumbled of into the darkness.

It was just a couple of roads back to our apartment. Kay was in a lovely mood. She was effervescent in her love for me. This was in her eyes, her words and in her touch. She was very relaxed and very happy. We were both very well oiled with alcohol but also very mellow. Arm in arm we waltzed across the Passeig de Joan de Borbon. There was little traffic about at this time of night. The occasional taxi was running up and down the near deserted road. As we crossed the road the Spar supermarket was busy. A group of late night revellers were buying more supplies and exhibited a very jovial mood. There were a few diners still eating in the outside areas of the many restaurants that formed the frontage of this road, although by the actions of the waiters it was easy to tell where they would rather be at this late hour. The dark sky was moonless but clear and full of stars, although as we walked along with our heads arched backwards we could see few of them through the neon haze provided by the shops and restaurants in front of us. We stepped into the relative darkness of the side streets. The tall apartment buildings either side of us rose up seemingly continuously into the dark sky. There were a few street lights that gave enough illumination for us to see where we were, but little more.

As we turned into Carrer Sant Miquel there was an unusual amount of noise coming from the right hand side of the road. Half way up the apartment block on probably the third floor, there was a party going on. Voices filled the street and echoed their importance. The apartment obviously covered most of the frontage of that particular block, as there were no other lights on apart from in the three windows of that floor. Each room was crammed with people. No music but lots of drink fuelled conversation. It must have been a fancy dress party of some kind as on the two balconies overlooking the dark street were four people dressed in a variety of guises. Batman was wretching over the side, comforted by a Kylie Minogue look-alike, on one balcony, whilst on the other, a guy dressed as Keanu Reeves out of the matrix was using his tongue to investigate the dentistry of Lieutenant O'Hoora from Star Trek. We looked up at the party and sensed the atmosphere. We smiled at each other, happy that we were as happy as the party people, and headed towards our apartment. As we approached the doorway to our block there was a shout from behind us:

"Look and you shall find. Find Ramon Turro and you will find your solution."
Kay and I turned immediately and looked high towards the source of the voice. It was hard to see clearly although it appeared that Batman and Kylie, Keanu and Lieutenant O'Hoora, had been replaced by a single white female. She was very white. She seemed to hover over the balcony. She had golden blonde long shoulder length hair and a white gown that covered all her body. What stunned us both visually was that she had wings. The light from the apartment shone brightly behind the figure and illuminated the wings. They didn't look like the usual pretend wings as they were enormous and filled the balcony. We both stared at the spectacle. The apparition then disappeared as the lights went off in the party apartment. There was a lot of confused shouting and disgruntled comments that quickly disappeared after a few seconds when the lights came back on. The figure on the balcony had gone. Both balconies were now empty. Kay looked up at the apartment.

"Charlie, I know I have drunk quite a lot tonight, but that was really an angel I saw wasn't it?"
I was dumbfounded. If ever there was such a thing as an angel we had just seen it.
"I don't know," I said.
"That was really weird. It's a fancy dress party but that did not look like a fancy dress angel."
"She was floating above the balcony.....and those wings...they looked real."
"Yeah. But it must have been fancy dress...... What did she say?"
"Something about 'Look and you shall find, look on Ramon Turro for your solution'. Mused Kay.
"Let's go and find that angel," I said forcibly. With that I held Kay by the hand and headed for the party apartment.

By now the party was in full swing and so it was easy to get in to the apartment. As we walked inside we were a little shocked by some of the behaviour. We're not at all prudish and are used to all kinds of action, but we were a little taken aback. There were about fifty people in the apartment that had three main rooms. It was a recently refurbished apartment with parquet flooring and exposed ceiling beams. The furniture was modern, probably IKEA, and minimalist. As we walked in to the hallway, we passed the toilet. The door was half open and there was a girl dressed as a prostitute leaning over the toilet as a huge man dressed as King Kong was entering her from behind. Sex is a beautiful thing but not, in my mind, when observed by others. The girl was making sounds so loud that everyone else had obviously moved away into the apartment. As we got into the main room everyone was standing apart from a couple of punk rockers who were slumped on a sofa sniffing a white powder. We were surprised. Drugs are a daily part of society and rarely do you see people doing drugs openly in amongst large numbers of people. The only good thing about this situation was that, despite the obviously high levels of alcohol consumed, there was an obvious disdain for the drug takers on the face of everyone within sight of them. As we moved through the room, squeezing between all kinds of weird and wonderful characters, we saw superman and bugs bunny grab the two drug abusers by the arm and march them out of the apartment. We could hear them being taken out to the street and sent on their drug fuelled way. When the two characters returned the assembled partygoers broke out into a spontaneous applause. The happy party atmosphere returned and the atmosphere was cranked up a notch.

We looked in every room twice. There was no sign of an angel.

Eventually, exhaustion told on us. Kay was finding it difficult to stay awake and I had suddenly gone all tired, as if my body had had all its energy pumped out of it. We stumbled out of the apartment into the street and across the road to our apartment block. My brown linen three quarter length trousers had a myriad of pockets many of which were double pockets. It took me awhile to locate the area of the key and then several more frustrating minutes where I struggled to release the key to the apartment block from my trouser pocket. While this was going on Kay fell asleep standing up and leaning against the doorway. I opened the door to the apartment block just as she was starting to fall backwards into the road. I grabbed her with my right arm and kept the door open with my left foot. She was quite heavy as a dead weight. I managed to hold on to her and direct her into the doorway. She came around slightly without moving her eyes. I pushed the button to light up the apartment and struggled to get Kay up the two flights of stairs. Her legs continued to move as I pushed her up the stairs from behind. At our apartment I steadied her and opened the door. I managed to guide her along through the hallway, the small living room, before helping her to flop onto the bed. I undressed her, with difficulty, covered her with the duvet and went back to the kitchen to get a drink of water for both of us. I turned all the lights off and placed the glasses of water on either side of the bed. I quickly undressed, strewing my clothes across the floor and climbed into bed next to Kay. Within seconds I was as fast asleep as Kay.

Chapter Twenty-Four

Pretence

Pretence

Life is what you make it. Life is full of surprises, disappointments and spurned aspirations. Whatever happens to you though, life is still what you make of it. Too many people live their life as a pretence. They live pretending to be something they are not. They live pretending to be something or someone they would like to be. These people are not happy. The secret to a happy life, is not fame or fortune, it is very simple. The secret to a happy life is to know and accept who you are. People who live their life as themselves are people we can all learn from.

August 1st 2005, 10 a.m – 1o1o, 104 Carrer Sant Miquel,, Barceloneta

"Come on wake up, wake up, you lazy English people!" Ferran was right above me shaking my arm vigorously. I woke in a panic, disorientated and confused. Where was I and why was this man shouting at me? Kay was much better at waking quickly and she was sitting up in bed quickly questioning Ferran.

"How did you get in here? What do you want that is so urgent?"
Ferran slouched back into the chair in the corner of the room. He looked terrible. He had he same clothes on he had had on the night before. Even then they had looked like he had lived in them for a couple of days, now they looked even worse. His hair was matted and needed a

wash and he was completely unshaven, probably had been for a couple of days.

"Go and take a shower in our bathroom. You look dreadful. You can borrow one of Charlie's shirts. While you do that we can get dressed and serve you up some coffee."
Kay laid the instructions down so clearly that Ferran dutifully got up and sloped off to the bathroom. Kay and I got up, dressed and got some breakfast together. We both felt fine after a couple of glasses of water. The smell of coffee soon filled the apartment as the coffee filter machine got to work.

Ferran emerged from the bathroom, clean-shaven, smelling fresh and looking ten times better than he had earlier. He was just wearing his trousers and was holding a towel to his hair.

"Here, wear this," said Kay as she threw him one of my shirts.
Ferran struck out his right arm and caught the flying shirt. He quickly put it on and sat down at the small white table in the main room of the apartment. In front of him was a cup of steaming coffee and a row of chocolate chunks. He looked at the chocolate in disbelief.
"That's all the food we have in. Eat it. You look like you need some energy." I said. Ferran picked up the chocolate at snapped off a chunk. As he ate it he slurped the hot coffee.
"Ahhh. Mocha," he laughed.
We sat quietly for a few minutes looking at each other and drinking coffee.
"What happened to you last night?" I questioned.
"After you left us?"

I knew the answer but I felt like teasing the detective. Before Ferran could answer I added to the original question.
"Is Detective Maria your new love?"
Ferran looked up from his coffee and smiled.

"The love you and Kay have is very special. Anyone who spends anytime with you both can feel the emotional energy and love that you transfer between each other. I have never experienced that kind of love."
He paused for thought.
"Maria though is certainly special. I like her a lot. She seems to like me and we get on with each other well and....excuse me for being a little graphic, Kay," he said as he looked respectfully towards her.
"....together we have great sex."
"So it was a good night last night?" jutted in Kay.
"You saw the way I looked when I came in."
Enough had been said on this matter.

Ferran was in an open, accessible mood. There was no doubt that he relaxed in our company. Something we both sensed that he rarely did. We doubted that he had many real friends. He was different and although he could socialise with anyone, he was a complex and reserved character. Kay and I were sufficiently different, removed from his normal reality and yet on the same wavelength as him to allow him to relax with us.
"I do really enjoy your company."
Ferran looked as us both as he spoke. His words confirmed our feelings. "Last night was really enjoyable. I feel I can be myself and relax. Which in this job I can rarely do. We must maintain this friendship after this investigation."

He looked Kay in the eyes and held firmly onto my hand. He held this position for a few moments. I released his grip and replied.

"We really enjoy your company Will. We are also keen to develop the friendship."

It was as if that was the signal he required to return to detective mode. In a nano-second he was back playing the detective.

"You are not in danger anymore. Our investigations lead us to believe that there is no interest in hurting you….what ever you find out. The people we are dealing with are not murderers, they are gentlemen financiers."

"What about the thugs that went for Jordi Badia." I protested.

"No problemo. No problemo. He was asking for it. I would have liked to bend his face a little … the little shit. He is not a nice person and he would have got what he deserved. Unfortunately I am policeman and I have to protect the public."

He looked up at the ceiling in despair.

"So…you two are safe. I know."

He stared at us both intently. Kay was tough but I could tell she wasn't convinced.

"I really didn't like it when we were abducted Will, why should we get involved further? What's in it for us?" she requested.

Detective Ferran took a few moments to answer. He stood up and slid open the door onto the small balcony. He stepped outside and lit a cigarette.

"I must give these things up. I do admire you English. Most of you don't smoke anymore."

Ferran was nervously trying to find the right words. The words flitted across his face as he tried out various approaches.

"You are right. But I sense that there is an element in both of you that wants to know what is going on in this particular situation. But, as you say.....you don't need to know. I want you to help me. I need you to help me. My superiors have obviously had pressure put on them to close this case. But my boss ...even though he's told me this, has also given the impression that he wants me to continue with it. He knows I will and that I don't care about the implications of authority. I am not a career policeman. I really want to see this case through. There is something big at the end of this I am sure. The problem I have is that they, the bad guys whoever they all are, know about me. Why else would they put pressure on me to desist? They know about you two too. But they think you are amateurs and have no influence or power. Remember, these people only understand power."

Kay looked across at me and reached out for my hand. I put my right hand in hers and squeezed it supportively.

"OK. We will help you," said Kay.

"But only because we like you and because, I am, in particular, very nosy!"

We all laughed.

Ferran spent several minutes outlining to us exactly what he wanted us to do. It sounded very easy. It sounded very safe. The problem was that we were working in a world that we really did not understand. Ferran wanted us to pretend to be something we weren't. It was interesting and potentially dangerous, with or without his assurances.

Chapter Twenty-Five

Deception

Engaño

Deception, an interesting word. A word that accounts for a great deal of human behaviour. A word that should be one of the words fully explained to children in their life skills classes. We are all very experienced and very good at deception, whether we admit it to ourselves or not. The vast majority of people don't realise that they are regularly deceiving themselves and other people with their words and actions. Deception is an unwitting art form in most human interactions.

August 1st 2005, 11.45 a.m – 1º1º, 104 Carrer Sant Miquel, Barceloneta

Kay and I were actually getting ourselves mentally prepared for some real life deception. Deception that we were fully aware of and that was planned and executed with the intention of eliciting information out of innocents. We sat in our apartment discussing everything that Detective Ferran had just outlined to us. We were up for the action but we were very apprehensive. Ferran had convinced us that we were no longer of interest to the people we were helping to investigate. Unfortunately the incident at the apartment of Jordi Badia was still very fresh in our minds.

Ferran had explained to us that one of his colleagues had spent some time looking closely at the piece of paper we had been given by Xavier Badia, the paper with the names of the members of FC La Llotja written on it. The paper had also had numbers scribbled in pencil next to the player's names. Ferran's colleague had immediately believed these numbers to be part of a code and she had subsequently spent a couple of days puzzled by it. Eventually she had realised that it spelt out a name. The numbers in pencil simply related to letters of the alphabet, with the two starred numbers referring to two actual numbers. The name the code spelt out was 'Ramon Turro 106'. This had surprised us both, as it had been the name that the angel had shouted out to us the night before. Kay believed the angel had fancied me and was just shouting out her address to encourage a visit from me. I hadn't felt that at all. I felt it was something more sinister, but as we couldn't track down the angel at the party we had had to agree to disagree.

Detective Ferran had no idea what was at Ramon Turro 106, but he did know that it was an address on a road in Poble Nou. He wanted us to visit the place and find out what, if anything, it had to do with FC La Llotja. We could tell from his demeanour and attitude that he didn't believe in the code breaking. He felt that it was a pure coincidence that the numbers spelt out the name of the road. All he had wanted us to do was to visit the address and find out who the owners were. We were to report back to him at 5 p.m that day at the '23 Beach Café'. Ferran had not wanted any of his departments' detectives to get further involved in this case openly. He was afraid that the whole case would be fully shut down if his superiors sensed that progress was being made, rather than the partial shut down that had been put in place.

Kay was apprehensive as we left our apartment at around 1 p.m. I could tell by her quiet mood that she was internally running over all the potential possibilities that might result from her actions. I worked in the same way. Everything I did was planned in my mind. I always ran over the worst-case scenario and planned a course of action for handling such a situation. I was already prepared for whatever might lie ahead for us today. I felt good. I felt like an athlete on the verge of winning a gold medal.

We walked over to the far side of the Ciutadella Parc to Carrer Wellington. This was one of our favourite streets in the whole city. As you looked towards the city the park was on the left. The sounds emanating from the city zoo that formed part of the park, gave this area a slightly surreal and tropical feel, particularly on a day like today when the sun was extremely hot. To the right of the road were some grand buildings, an old, soon to be renovated apartment block, a tall building that formed part of a Library for the University and some half-built, brand new strangely designed buildings for the University. The main feature of Carrer Wellington though was an avenue of trees that lined a grass filled tramline. Trams ran from here up to the Gran Via, a route Kay and I often took for an early evening drink out of town. The trams were very modern, very clean and driver less.

As we walked along Carrer Wellington we soaked up the atmosphere of this lovely road whilst looking for Carrer Ramon Turro that, we knew from our map, ran off from this road. I looked down at the tarmac we were walking on and remained amazed at how it showed no sign of melting despite the intense heat of the day. Kay offered me a drink from the water bottle she was carrying. The two litre bottle was already nearly empty.

"It's really slow progress in this heat." observed Kay.

"I hope number 106 is this end of Ramon Turro!"

"There it is," I pointed as we approached the intersection between Wellington and Ramon Turro. I held Kay's hand as we headed for the pavement on Ramon Turro.

"I wonder who Ramon Turro was?"
I mused as we sauntered along the road searching with our eyes for any numbers of buildings. Kay ignored my question.
"Look." Kay said.
"That's number 18. It can't be far."
Our pace quickened with the satisfaction that we were not far from our target destination.

Before long we were standing outside one of the odd looking industrial buildings that made up the majority of the urban landscape around this part of Barcelona. The buildings were a mixture of old, oldish and newish. They were all shapes and sizes. They were used for all kinds of purposes, from homes to motor repair shops. Just above a very old and tatty stone doorway that stood to the left of the two-storey building in front of us, was a bronze plaque. It was very old and the once deeply inscribed lettering was severely tarnished making it very hard to read. The plaque was only about half a metre square. Kay and I were both keen to see what secrets this address on Carrer Ramon Turro held. We both instinctively stepped quickly forward to read the plaque. Even when we were right underneath it the writing was still extremely hard to read. I stood on the top of the two small steps that lay in front of the doorway. I stretched forward and upward with my left arm and rubbed the brass plaque with my hand. Immediately, the tarnish started to recede. Kay handed me a tissue. I took hold of it and rubbed it fiercely over the writing on the plaque. We both stood back as the words on the plaque were gradually revealed to us, 'La Hermandad Del Noveno Noviembre, s.a."

"Well I really didn't expect that," extorted Kay.
"I thought they were a secret organisation. I wonder what this building is?"

I was still looking with real interest at the brass plaque. "I can only think that this is the office that manages their properties. If it is, then some of the Brotherhood must be involved in current goings on. Looking at the sign though, it must be a very small and quiet operation. They really can't get many visitors."
"I think you're right. There must be information in this building about the brotherhood though," suggested Kay.
"Some perhaps, but I doubt there is much, if anything, to implicate the members of the Brotherhood."
Kay was looking really fired up and her intelligence was radiating from her.
"Ferran said the code pointed to this address and the angel pointed us here. Also, although details of the Brotherhoods financial dealings were meant to be associated with our apartment, they weren't. Perhaps this is just another deception. Perhaps the best way to cover up their work was to actually set up a company and an office."
"I think you may be right," I said repetitively.

We stood back in the quiet road. There was absolutely no action. We could see no-one and apart from a lonely car dashing past an intersection there was no movement. There were a couple of parked cars a little way down the road but nothing else. The building itself looked drab and dull even in the sparkling sunlight. It was non-descript 1960's building with no style. There were just about two stories to the building, although it was quite low in height. Apart from a window on the first floor and a door at ground level it was a pretty unremarkable building.
"I reckon we could find things we need in that building," I asserted nodding my head in its direction.
"Yes but.......'," cautioned Kay.
"Yes but what," I queried.
"Yes but what if we are caught?"

"Look, there is no-one around and anyway, we're working for the police!"' I countered.
Kay wasn't at all convinced but I sensed that she was prepared to give it a go.
"Ok, but stay together and don't do any damage," she cautioned.
With that comment I held her hand and walked towards the front entrance. I really didn't know how we would get into the building although the most obvious route, through the front door, was worth a try.
I grabbed the metal handle of the heavy glass panelled door. I pulled it and as I did so I nearly fell over backwards as the door flew open. We paused, looked inside and then slowly and carefully edged into the inner hallway of the building.

Chapter Twenty-Six

Intrigue

Encanto

People increasingly like to be in control of their lives. A recent quote by Soshana Zuboff always sticks in my mind:

"We want our voices to be heard. We want control over our lives. This is a fundamental shift in social maturity that has been about five decades in the making, and is now having an explosive effect on the way we think of ourselves as citizens, as employees, as consumers."

This is seemingly, perfectly true. We all want to do what we want and yet we also want someone to blame if things go wrong. This element of control leaves no room for intrigue. One definition of intrigue is a situation when we are: 'caused to be interested or curious'. Such a mental state can only be good for a longer life as the more there is to think about the better the chance you have of avoiding dementia.

August 1st 2005, 3 p.m – Carrer de Ramon Turro

Intrigue was a good word to describe how Kay and I felt as we stepped into Carrer de Ramon Turro, 106. The building looked a little odd from the outside and was equally strange on the inside. We both stood inside a very small entrance area and quietly closed the door behind us. There was door right in front of us with an iron meshed single glass panel. It was white and had a bolt attached to a metal bracket. The door looked like an access to a storeroom. The floor and walls of the hallway were matching green. The carpet was a plain green and the walls a lighter shade. There was only one way for us to go.

“Let's just pretend we are looking for somewhere and that this was the only place open.” Kay suggested.
“Fine.” I replied, using a word our daughter Susie used often, meaning “OK, I’ll go along with it but I’m not particularly happy about it.”
“Look confused, harassed and lost,” instructed my wife.
This wasn’t hard to do, as I was feeling particularly tentative about going up the stairs. The stairs took us to the first floor of the building where the corridor they led onto quickly branched to the right. Ahead of us there was another single glass panelled door. This time we could see through it and there was a light on in the room it opened into. As we stealthily approached the door we could see more of the room behind it. It looked like an open plan office with three desks and a number of filing cabinets. We stopped at the door and peered through the window in it.

“Can you see anybody?” I quizzed Kay.
We were both struggling to get our heads into position for us to see all of the room behind the door.
“Not a soul. But look.” Kay pointed.
“Those two desks are covered in papers and both the computer screens are still on. There must be somebody in there. Look. There’s another door leading off the back of the room.”
“C’mon. Let’s go in.” I said bravely.
With that I pushed the door open and we burst into the office. Kay was right. The room was being worked in. The phone was ringing, the air conditioning unit was at full blast and there was a jacket on the back of one of the desk chairs.

"Hola!" Kay shouted, gently at first.
"Hola! Hola!" she repeated.
"Esta aqui?"
There wasn't a sound. The phone had stopped and the air conditioning unit had briefly switched itself off for a deserved rest. We stood listening in the middle of the room for a few minutes, looking around all parts of the room and glancing nervously back at each other. I tried the door at the far end of the office that had only taken four or five of my strides to reach.
"Anything?" asked Kay hopefully.
"No, it's just a back flight of stairs."
I stepped fully back into the room and looked at one of the active computer screens.
"Let's see if we can find anything. There's no-one here and I am sure we would hear anyone coming up either staircase. You look in the filing cabinets and I'll look on here." I suggested sitting down at the desk.

After several minutes of joyless investigation, Kay opened up one of the lower drawers on the older of the filing cabinets. She skimmed through the file headings with her fingers.
"I've found something Charlie.....come here!"
I rushed over to join her at the rear of the office. Kay was now kneeling down carefully looking at the file contents in front of her.
"These front five files are all the properties the Brotherhood is currently looking to purchase. The next nine or ten are for properties they already own, and......the few files at the back are for properties they used to own."
"Let's look at the older ones first." I suggested.
Kay pulled a few files out hurriedly. We were very aware of the trouble we would be in if we were caught.
"All these are properties in streets around Bogatell. Where is that?" Kay queried.

"I'm sure it's around here, you would think so wouldn't you."
"This one has got an old map attached to it," observed Kay.
"I think you're right. There's the Ciutadella Parc."
Kay pointed to what was clearly the park with her index finger of her right hand.
"Look. There used to be railway lines between this area and the sea. It looks totally different to the layout today."
"Yes. All these properties, about twenty of them were owned by the Brotherhood between 1977 and 1984. They are all in the Bogatell area between here and the railway lines."
Kay was rapidly interpreting the files in front of her.
"These are all copies of deeds."
She held several files in her hands as she spoke.
"I don't understand the Spanish but look at the names where the deeds are signed. These three are all the same."
Kay pointed at each deed in turn. We felt sure that this was the kind of information we needed to find for Ferran.
"Notario – Santiago Lines, Signatorias, a nombre de la Brotherhood – Julian Solbes, Jordi Badia, Raul Martinez and Jordi Torres."

Suddenly we heard a loud crash as the door downstairs through which we had entered some ten minutes earlier slammed open. Hurried steps started up the staircase.
"Quick, quick, put them back."
Kay was one step ahead of me and had the files back in the cabinet drawer and it shut before I could finish telling her what to do. I rushed over to the computer screen and switched it back to the home screen. Within seconds we were standing nonchalantly in the centre of the office politely waiting. Inside our hearts were racing and we were sweating profusely as we waited for someone to come crashing through the door.

Chapter Twenty-Seven

Burning Desires

Deseos Que se queman

There are times in life when you just cannot wait to do something or you cannot wait for a much anticipated event to happen. Such burning desires are adrenalin filled experiences and well worth going through. Sometimes though, the meaning of a word or phrase can be totally misleading.

August 1st 2005, 3.15 p.m – Carrer de Ramon Turro

We waited for an expected entrance by someone, our eyes on the door. Suddenly, we heard a whoosh noise. It took us no time to realise what was going on. We could see the flames through the window rushing towards the doorway. The hot air hit the door and was temporarily rebuffed. We were momentarily shocked. Neither of us had expected this. As smoke started to seep through the gaps at the side of the door we became alert to the need to take some action.

"The other stairs." I shouted as I grabbed Kay's arm and turned towards the rear of the office. Before we moved a step towards the door we could see an orange glow growing in size around the outline of the door. As we stared in disbelief, the smoke started to ooze into the office from around the door frame.

"What do we do?" I questioned, looking urgently around the room and the back to Kay. She had a scared but determined look on her face. Kay was a real survivor and could always be relied upon in times of panic. She didn't say a great deal in such situations, instead her brain processed all possibilities in the search for a solution to the problem. Kay was very different to me, although I, too, didn't panic. Instead, I talked incessantly, running through everything going through my mind.

"We need to get out of here. The smoke is starting to fill the room. It won't be long before we can't breathe. What about the windows? We could smash them with the furniture."
"Don't worry Charlie. We are on the first floor and we can just open the window with the latch. Look."
Kay pointed to the large windows and their easy opening mechanisms. Kay was right. Perhaps we weren't in as much danger as I had thought. Despite the advancing flames and quickly amassing smoke we had a way out. As we moved towards the window we heard an unusual hissing sound coming from the rear office stairwell. The hissing was getting louder and more pronounced.
"It's the sound of an extinguisher," observed Kay.
"There's someone coming."
At that moment a tall, black haired woman burst in through the door.
"Esta bien, esta bien?" She shouted.
As she saw us the look of concern disappeared from her face.
"Bueno, bueno. Follow me. Pronto."
The woman was tall for a Spanish woman. Her hair was well groomed and shoulder length and her face revealed a young thirty-something. She wore an all denim outfit with a white t-shirt that was rapidly changing to grey. The extinguisher she held in her hand was obviously heavy, although she used it to great effect. The flames that had been racing up the rear stairwell were greatly subdued. She hurried back down the steps, spraying the white foam

as she went. Kay quickly followed, closely pursued by me.

We stood outside the building having emerged at the back of the building and worked our way back onto the Carrer de Ramon Turro. The flames had taken hold of the building and were racing to the ceiling inside the office. We watched the performance from the safety of the road. The dancing flames bounced against the closed window. Suddenly the window cracked and exploded and the flames leapt out of their enclosure and started to climb up the outside of the building onto the roof. Sirens gave us advance warning of the imminent arrival of the fire brigade, although the speed of the conquest of the building by the fire gave little hope for any salvage. The building was low and slightly separate from other buildings. There was obviously no other life in there to be rescued.

"Conchita Pedralbes-Carew," announced our rescuer.

"Pleased to meet you, Senor and Senora Lowson."

We were very pleased to meet her, but we were immediately confused by her knowledge of us.

"Thank you very much for rescuing us. You were very heroic." said a relieved Kay.

All three of us were still panting as our hearts struggled to calm each of us down after the unwanted excitement of the past few minutes.

"Really heroic," I added.

"Thank you so much."

Kay had a black smoke grained glow to her face and her hair was singed in places from the heat as we had escaped down the stairwell. God knows what as mess I looked but I could feel the red glow of my skin and see the black soot on my arms. I was sweating badly and my hair was wet and matted.

Conchita looked us up and down. She had relaxed and was starting to smile.
“You two lead exciting life. You would have got out……out window. I pleased to help however.” Her English was good but stilted.
“”Come….we need to get out of here.”
The sirens were getting much louder and the flames stronger. Conchita led us towards a black Peugeot parked a little way along the road. I glanced back at the building that was now blackened by the flames that were still leaping out of the window. A huge plume of smoke was now rising into the sky vertically in the clear, still weather conditions. As we slowly walked away from the burning scene there was a stream of people coming out of buildings to get a better view of the excitement. The previously deserted street was rapidly filling with people. I glanced down at Kay’s trousers and saw a piece of smouldering debris rapidly eating into the flimsy material. I slapped her legs to douse the burning ember. All three of us looked at our clothes to check for anymore offending fragments from the fire.

We reached the car and Conchita flicked open the car locks with her zapper key. At this point a fire engine rushed into the street and quickly ground to a halt outside the blazing building. As the firemen leapt into action we hurried inside the car and Conchita steered us quickly off into the industrial grid of roads around Poble Nou. Kay and I sat in the back of the car smouldering as Conchita entertained us with her personality and confident broken English.
“You wondering how I know you , yeah?”
We were still dazed.
“I come here out of Uruguay……dos..two anos past. I love Barcelona. I have family no here though. Detective Ferran he like my work.”

Suddenly we started to understand. We were sitting in the rear of the car stunned by another near death experience in this very unusual week we were having. In reality we were a long way from real danger and could easily have jumped out of the window to safety. But to, two control obsessed professionals, such dangerous incidents just do not happen on a regular basis. It was a gradual realisation of where we were and what kind of situation we were involved in. The mention of Detective Ferran tuned us into Conchita's conversation.

"So, how do you know Ferran," I asked.

"I work in his office.....I come dos anos....later...I with no work. He meet and give me work."

"So did he talk about us? How do you know about us? Isn't his work confidential?" Kay had many questions.

"I very intelligent. I graduate...University Montevideo...forensic science."

It was easy to see what Ferran had seen in Conchita. She was increasingly attractive as her personality took hold of us. She was laughing and smiling and talked incessantly. Kay and I were relaxing rapidly in the aura of her personality. We both fell in love with her as a complete person.

"I work on clues...Ferran talks to me. I give ideas. I crack code with Brotherhood."

"Ramon Turro 106?" I questioned.

"Si, si, si," she laughed. "Esta mi."

Conchita was laughing now and trying to speak but finding it difficult. Her private joke was making it difficult for her to concentrate on the road.

"Ha, ha, ha......I was the angel. The white angel!" She roared.

We were dumbstruck. Kay looked at Conchita with disbelieving eyes. I was staring at the back of her jet, black hair.

"The angel on Carrer Sant Miquel? The white angel?" I asked.
"Yeeeesssss," she chortled.
"Yes, I was it. I put white all over me."
"Why?" Asked Kay.
"I need to get you to go to Ramon Turro. Ferran ...not sure of code. He not want to believe I code. I wanted you do it."
Conchita was a very clever woman. She had a hunch, cracked a code and had to make things happen.
"Why didn't you get into Raymon Turro yourself?" I queried.
"Detective Ferran told us, I need not be involved."
With that the car hurtled to a halt outside the Arts Hotel at the Port Olympic on the Barcelona seafront.

Chapter Twenty-Eight

Enlightenment

Aclaración

Religion is an essential belief system to the essential basic human being. Religion has always given people belief and a reason for living. There are loads of religions, all competing for their share of humanity. You can even make up your own religion and develop a lucrative following if you are savvy enough. Increasingly though, humans are eschewing the need for religious belief. The one religion that non-believers are sometimes vaguely attracted to is Buddhism - the religion that strives for personal enlightenment. This makes a lot of sense. The people in life who are happiest are those who have achieved a sense of personal enlightenment. Such people are few and far between, although very, very occasionally we all get a sense of what real enlightenment might be like.

August 1st 2005, 4.15 p.m – 23 Beach Café, Barceloneta

The weather was turning. The heat of the last few days had built up the air pressure and the sky was turning purple. Sitting at the 23 beach café on the Barceloneta beach Kay, Conchita and I looked along the beach past Frank Gerry's wonderful bronze fish sculpture towards Poble Nou. Smoke was still blackening the sky lightly from the fire we had witnessed at first hand although the deep darkness of the sky was primarily a result of the impending thunder. Rain was falling some miles along the coast and rapidly moving our way. A cool wind swept the beach ahead of the advancing rain. The beach was quickly clearing. People were picking up their towels and beachmats and hurrying into the grid of Barceloneta. We stayed put. We were under a canopy in the centre of the bar seating area.

If Conchita were worldwide ambassador for the Uraguayan nation, they would be the most popular people on the planet. Her personality was electric. She was really attractive because of her lovely persona. She made Kay and I feel really good about ourselves and made us feel really good about being friends with her. She was polite, funny, wise and modest, although she was also totally enlightened. She wanted a life of challenge, fun and happiness. Money wasn't important to her, but she wanted to learn and to meet people. We felt that we would be friends with her for life.

The beers had been flowing although Conchita had persuaded us to sample some exquisite, but by Spanish standards, expensive Spanish wine. We were well oiled as Ferran arrived.
"Hola, mi amigos!"
"Hola!" We replied in universal triumph.
Ferran sat down at our table and stared at the three of us. After a few minutes of silence the skies made us jump. A huge roll of thunder filled the air and a fork of lighting lit up the power station at Besos. We all jumped into life.
"You look terrible." Ferran said as he completed his observation of our dishevelled and burnt state.
"What have you all been doing?"
"I'm too tired and have drunk too much to tell you Detective Ferran. I'm sure Conchita has the energy to fill you in on our afternoon of excitement," replied Kay before snuggling into my chest with her head.
Conchita was still vibrant and as the rain hammered down around the beach café, which provided impenetrable screen, she quickly ran through the activities on Ramon

Turro. Ferran looked across to us when Conchita had finished.
"So? What did you find out?"
He knew we would not have left the burnt out building empty handed.
"How do you know? You are right. We have found what you need." I said.
"The Brotherhood seemed to have brought lots of properties in the Bogatell area before the Olympic development. Santiago Lines has made sure that Julian Solbes is a signatory to everything."
"The documents….you have them?" queried Ferran.
"No, we were too keen to escape the building," answered Kay.
"But….all we saw were copies of deeds. There must be a registry office in Barcelona with the original deeds."
"Si. There is a registry office. We must research this. Solbes is an important politician. I am sure that he would have had contacts or influence on the many committees that prepared the city for the Olympics. …..If he had known about the need for the land along the coast then he would have been aware of the potential to make millions of pesetas for the sale of that land. We need to find out which committees he was a member of." commented Ferran.
"We have a problem though."
Stated Ferran, as he suddenly became more serious and thoughtful. The rain was now beginning to ease off. The thundering of it on the top of the narrow canopy of the beach bar was relenting and it was now much easier to hear what each other was saying. The twenty or so people still at the bar began to spread out a little as the rain eased. The beach was almost deserted, save for a few hardy, stupid or drunk souls who were still lying on the sodden sand. As the rain eased a gentle steam rose from the beach as the heat started to return.

"What problem?" Kay questioned.
"Someone knew you were in the offices at Ramon Turro."
"How?" I snapped.
"You mean that someone tried to kill us?"
"No….I think it was a little warning. I also think that they had to destroy the deeds…the evidence."
"How do you know this?" Kay repeated.
"Jeffe Inspector Delgado came to see me before I left the office and told me about the fire at some important offices in Poble Nou. He wanted to know if I knew anything about it."
"What did you say?" I asked.
"The truth." He smiled.
"I said that I had no idea what was going on there and that I didn't even know what place he was talking about. But, I know he knew there was something going on."
Conchita was thinking about what Ferran had just said. She took another swig from her beer and radiated an enormous smile across the table. We were all drawn in.
"No-one notice me or know me in office," she revealed.
"I just anoder Uruguayan."
We looked and waited for what was coming next.
"I look into Olympic committees…I very good researcher….no..Detective Ferran? I right about Ramon Turro, no?"
She smiled. Ferran looked deep into his drink.
"And you two," she continued pointing Kay and I out with her deep, dark eyes.
"You two need to investigate registry…find deeds….get copies…evidence. We need keep Ferran out of it." She was right.

Ferran had other work to do, and the tasks were allotted amongst the three of us and we went our separate ways. Kay and I hurried across the wide Barceloneta esplanade as the sun was beginning to break through. We needed a shower, but we most of all needed to get our heads together to find out where the Registry Office was and to get the information we needed. We arranged to meet the other two at the same time the next day at Bar Colombo.

I love hot places after a really heavy storm. The streets were cleansed, the air was washed through and the smells were fresh and, I found, exhilarating. We walked the few blocks through Barceloneta back to our apartment. I opened the heavy metal door to the apartment block and stepped inside. It wasn't dark outside but the windowless apartment stairwell was in the shade. I clicked on the light. We fell into our apartment. The air was heavy; it hadn't been cleansed by the outdoor rain. As we stood in the small narrow hallway we caught our reflections in the mirror. We both started laughing simultaneously. We were tired and had again been scared, but we were getting used to it. We felt part of an increasingly strong and supportive team and we were making as many new friends as enemies. It was obvious to us both that we were in this incident for the duration and we might as well enjoy it as much as we could.

"You look dreadful." laughed Kay.

"But I look ten times worse."

We were soot covered, sweat ridden, wet and dirty. We both rushed through our showers. As I waited for Kay to finish her shower, I lay naked on the bed reading the telephone directory that Kay had acquired a few days ago, looking for an address for the land registry. After several minutes Kay, cleansed and smelling beautiful came into the bedroom and lay on the bed next to me. She knelt on all fours and ran her tongue from my ankle up my shin and along my thigh. I knew where she was going and my anticipation grew.

Chapter Twenty-Nine

Bewilderment

Desconcierto

I've always wondered what exactly goes through the brain of a pheasant when having dashed across the road in front of a speeding car, as it looks around to stare imminent death in the face. The look of total bewilderment in the face of such a stupid creature is perhaps not surprising, but when you see it in a human it is a little less so.

August 1st 2005, 8.15 p.m – Carrer Sant Miquel 104, 1.1., Barceloneta

As we came down the stairs from our apartment Kay casually checked the battered metal post box that just about hung on the wall near the iron grilled front door. We rarely got post; if we did they were bills or flyers. She could see a letter through the metal grill.
"I'll just nip back and get the key." she said as she hurried back up to the apartment to get the key to the post box. It wasn't long before we were out in the street with a letter in Kay's hand. Kay quickly ripped it open. The outside of it had our names and address typed on it. It wasn't a bill. Kay took out a sheet of light blue paper. There was an address on the top right of a place somewhere in Barcelona in a district we hadn't been to or even heard of. We stood in the middle of Carrer Sant Miquel in the fading sunlight side by side reading the hand written words:

My Dear Senor and Senora Lowson,

We feel that we know you well even though we do not know you well. We must first apologise for any discomfort or upset that our actions have already or will cause you. Please believe us when we say that we are committed to your safety although our actions we believe are necessary.

We know a great deal about you and indeed about Detective Ferran, your friend. We know we can trust you to act in the interests of fairness and justice. You have, through no fault of your own, become embroiled in the affairs of La Hermandad del Noveno Noviembre. You could have walked away, but we know that you, like us want to see an end to the wrongs that have been committed. We know that you will find the source of these wrongs to be Julian Solbes and that you will, with Detective Ferran, find the evidence and means to bring him to justice.

Rest assured we will do everything in our power to support you. We have some very incriminating evidence of our own which we will bring to light soon.

We will meet again.

Kay and I read this letter with fascination. We could not think who it was from. When we saw the signatures at the bottom of the letter we both stumbled backwards in shock and bewilderment. We were both momentarily taken aback. It was signed by, Jesus Antich and Josep Lluis Alvaro.

"They are dead." I gasped.

"I can't believe it," Kay gawped, her eyes staring fixatedly at the signatures on the paper.

"Wait," she said as she fumbled with the envelope in her hand.

"July 31st…the letter was posted on July the 31st…look at the postmark." Kay insisted pointing at it with her finger. I looked.
"Yes, but they died on the 30th July."
"They must have posted it late on the 30th just after they had met us, or got someone else to post it for them."
This made a lot of sense. In fact it was the only sensible explanation.
"I think you're right…but it's very spooky receiving such a supportive letter from two dead men." I said.
"Yes, but doesn't it make you want to see this through to the end. They are right, or so Ferran thinks. This Julian Solbes guy is bad news. It gives me real strength," Kay said with real feeling.
I held her hand and shoved the letter into the back pocket of the cut off trousers I was wearing. We headed for the little restaurant at the end of our block, Passatemps, we were too tired to go much further tonight.

Passatemps was a local restaurant always accessible to tourists. It was cheap and alternated between being full and nearly empty. The food, when the chef was there, was very good, although you could never tell. The owner, or manager, was a laid back guy in his thirties who seemed to go into a mild panic every time he had a customer for food. This panic often resulted in him making a hurried phone call and a few minutes later a chef, or kitchen hand, appearing to satisfy our needs.

We started with a couple of well-deserved beers. The first beer is always the best and within minutes we had both devoured it. Kay ordered some food and a bottle of house red. I really loved the way she rolled off the words, 'una bottella de vino tinto de la casa'. We quickly forgot about the letter and started to plan our next course of action. We couldn't find any sign of the registry office, probably as it was called something very different in Spanish or Catalan. Kay then had the brilliant idea to call our friend, Roma Bosch.

Roma was the solicitor we had used last year when buying our apartment. He was actually a partner in a law firm and was a lawyer dealing in company law. From the moment we had first met him we knew we had many things in common. We had only met him a few times but little by little our friendship had grown. Roma was an attractive, handsome, forty year old. He was extremely clever and could speak Catalan, Spanish, French and English fluently. He looked younger than he was and, one of the reasons we got on so well was that he had a very English, self-deprecatory sense of humour. Roma and I also both loved football. Barca F.C was Roma's passion. He had been a rising star for them when he was eighteen but a terrible injury had smashed his kneecap ending a promising career. Ever since then he made it his job to know everything and anything about the club. He had a citywide reputation for this knowledge. When we had first met I couldn't believe that he remembered the time Aston Villa, the team I supported, played Barcelona, with Johann Cruyff et al, back in the 1980's.

I phoned Roma. We arranged to meet for lunch next day. We would meet him outside his offices on Diputacio, just off Passeig de Gracia.

Chapter Thirty

Inside Knowledge

Conocimiento Interior

No matter how hard you work, how hard you try and how much you think about things, sometimes there is just a huge impenetrable wall in front of you and your ambitions. At such times you need to be able to find a way around it and the easiest way is often to us the assistance of someone with real expertise or who has inside knowledge.

August 2nd 2005, 1 p.m – Carrer Dipacio, Central Barcelona

When we had hit a brick wall with our search for the registry building, Kay had instantly thought of Roma. The offices to Roma's law firm were quite hard to find. They were just along from Passeig de Gracia, one of the very smart shopping streets in Barcelona. Last year when we first came to meet Roma, we spent some time looking for the number to the building and the entrance. Eventually we had gambled on a dusty looking gateway, sealed by a large, arched double door. As soon as we had gone inside we realised we were in the right place as the company was listed and the building was very grand and decked in plush marble. Today we waited downstairs in the marble flooded entrance area.

We both heard the lift ping as it arrived on the ground floor. We looked up the short but wide stairway to wards the lift. Roma appeared, saw us, and smiled.
"Hola, good to see you again."

We exchanged pleasantries and basic news before heading off towards a restaurant Roma had booked.

We sat down at a window table, tucked away in the corner of a restaurant called 'Citrus'. The restaurant was on the second floor, had good views over the shoppers of Passeig de Gracia and was full of lunching business types. We ordered and settled down to a lovely bottle of Puntos red.
"Tell me then," started Roma.
"This is more than just a social get-together?"
"Well, yes, it is." I countered.
"You know you said that if we ever needed your help, to get in touch?"
"Yes," said Roma with cautious interest.
"Well……" I replied.
We continued to tell Roma about our adventures and ongoing needs. He listened with interest, carefully digesting and analysing the information we gave him.
"I am a very rational man, I have to be." He revealed after taking a quick sip of his wine.
"And the rational, careful solicitor man in me tells me not to get involved." He paused looking very serious. A smile then broke out across his face.
"But, you know. I am very good at what I do but I want more. I write thrillers. Maybe I could use your experiences in my writing. I also really like you two…. We have much in common. But the main reason for my decision to help you is my hatred for Julian Solbes."
With that statement the smile left his face.
"You know him?" asked Kay.
"Oh, yes. I have met him on several occasions, once or twice in court. He is a bully, very arrogant and he claims he has the interests of Catalonia at heart but he does not. He has only his interests at heart. I will help you." Roma was defiant and committed.

It was intriguing for Kay and me. Everyone we had met over the past few days had an intense dislike for this man, Julian Solbes. What was he like? We had no idea what he looked like or what his character was like. Yet, at the same time there are many people who are spellbound by him and in his control. Increasingly we wanted to meet him, to make up our own minds about the man. We knew though that Roma was a very good judge of character and that he was very tolerant. Julian Solbes must then be a very dangerous man.

"You are wonderful Roma," said Kay as she leant forward and planted a huge kiss on his cheek. Roma looked slightly embarrassed.
"What do you want me to do?"
"All we need you to look into Roma, is to find out the ownership of properties along Ramon Turro, and other roads in the Bogatell area of Barcelona, before the land was compulsorily purchased for the Olympics. We need you to find documents which implicate the Brotherhood and particularly Julian Solbes." I replied.
"Yes, but we must make sure that no one suspects your research. As you know, Julian Solbes is very powerful and he, through his associates, must be watching us." Kay spoke and we all looked carefully and furtively around us to see who was listening or watching. No-one appeared at all interested in what we were saying, although our waiter was a perpetual pest, moving and replacing our cutlery and glassware constantly.
"I know how we can make this happen," suggested Roma. "I will use one of our trainee solicitors, Jaume, you have met him."
"Oh yes, he speaks very good English," I replied.
"Yes, Jaume can do research for a case. That way no-one will think anything is out of the ordinary. Give me a day or so and I will get you the information you need."

Roma stood up. He brushed his suit down to straighten it out.
"I will phone you tomorrow."
He kissed Kay on the cheek and shook my hand.
"I must go back to work. You two are on holiday. Stay and enjoy another bottle of Puntos." With that statement he held the empty bottle up and signalled for another from the waiter.
"I will pay for this meal, the next one is on you two." Roma smiled and left the restaurant.
Kay and I settled into our seats with a real sense of satisfaction and attacked the new bottle of Puntos.

It was by now about two-thirty. We hadn't achieved a great deal today but the day had been less frenetic. As we worked our way through the second bottle of red there was no doubt that our waiter was getting increasingly agitated. Kay and I watched him carefully. As Roma had left he was obviously torn between following him or staying with us. After 20 minutes or so he was obviously regretting his decision to stay with us. We were gradually sinking further and further into our seats as the wine began to take effect. The waiter was under real pressure. He was sweating profusely and spent as much time around our table as he could. Unfortunately for him he learnt nothing from our conversations as we spent most of the conversation discussing the highlights and lowlights of the behaviours of the people we worked with.

After another half hour we decided to leave. The restaurant had by now emptied significantly and we sensed that the waiters were keen to see us go. Our waiter was particularly agitated and we were not surprised to see him follow us out of the building. Kay was feeling particularly flippant and free and easy. She told me that she had her 'magic credit card' and so we could look in one or two of her favourite clothes stores. We did feel that this would be an interesting test for our interested waiter.

At four p.m we had seen a great deal of Zara and Mango and decided to move on towards our meeting with Ferran. Kay had brought a wonderful pair of pink high-heeled shoes and a nice pair of jeans from Zara. Carrying our spoils we easily crept passed our dozing tracker, the waiter who had opted to watch from outside the stores rather than keep us in his sights. We had been so long in the two stores that he had obviously lost the will to live and was happily looking at the flow of people along the busy shopping street. Kay and I kept him in our sights as we disappeared into the melee and sneaked off down a side street. We headed for Bar Colombo.

Chapter Thirty-One

The Future

El futuro

The future is about skills, capabilities and knowledge. We are in a world where knowledge is important, but only as a basis to support one's creativity and actions. Knowledge is becoming a very useful tool and the acquisition of knowledge a very important skill. Conchita had many skills, the acquisition of knowledge being a really strong area of her repertoire.

August 2nd 2005, 4 p.m – Bar Colombo, Barceloneta

Conchita had a large purple folder in front of her sitting on the table in a near empty Bar Colombo. The chairs and tables outside were all inhabited, but inside, only a few Spanish people enjoyed a cold beer in the air-conditioned haven. The folder matched some quite wonderful purple earrings that dangled uncontrollably from Conchita's ears. They twizzled and turned with a mind of their own and due to their size your eyes looked at nothing else even when she started talking. Kay and I sat opposite her and signalled for three more beers.

Conchita was excited. Before she said anything she had her purple folder open and was taking several typed pieces of paper out which she placed in front of us. Kay picked up the first sheet. I looked at it from across her right shoulder. It was a list of committees and action groups set up to manage the lead up to the 1992 Olympic games that were held in Barcelona. The list was in Spanish but it was easy to tell what the headings were for. There was an initial list showing a number of groups that

had developed in order to bid for the Olympics and out of these, obviously following a successful bid, were lists showing the range of different committees set up to plan and manage the Olympics. The next few sheets revealed the names of the members of these committees.
"You've been busy," congratulated Kay.
Conchita was radiant. She looked better every time I saw her. She was extremely talented and was wasted in the menial roles she was generally given. Ferran had obviously spotted her talents and was utilising them.
"Si, I have found much out." she replied before launching into a full description of her findings.
"Look at these," she pushed more papers in front of us.
"I grouped the names of people on committees. You see names." She pointed at a particular sub group. The group of names she highlighted were familiar to us and her list showed five or six committees that each person was linked to.
"Julian Solbes….he was on six committees, Xavier Badia…four committees, Salvador Camps…five committees and Jordi Torras…six committees." I noticed.
"Yes, look at committees of Solbes."
Conchita pointed half way down the page.
"They are all do with land and development of land."
She was right. Every committee that Solbes was involved in was connected with planning, purchase and development of land for the Olympics. The Brotherhood had obviously spread themselves around the development groups to attract as much personal influence as possible.
"This doesn't show any real wrong doing though Conchita. Really, he could say he was helping Barcelona to develop." queried Kay.
Conchita was getting agitated and excited. She hadn't touched her new beer. She had a confident, almost smug look on her face as she drew even more papers out of her file.

"I go further," she said triumphantly, "….and I found this."
She placed a wadge of papers on the table in front of us. The papers were in detailed Spanish but it was obvious from their headings that they were minutes from meetings.
"These minutes from meetings of committees."
"Where did you get these?" Kay asked with an approving smile.
"On BCN city computer system. Good records. They say many things. It clear Solbes knew where main areas of development would be before Brotherhood buy property in Bogatell.'.
"She is very good, is she not?"
Detective Ferran announced from over the shoulder of Conchita. We had been so engrossed in what she was telling us we did not notice him arrive. With him was Detective Maria Fernandez Tupelo. They both looked good. They also looked good together. They were working closely together but their body language revealed a real chemical reaction that was taking place between them at the moment.

Before long the five of us were all fully up to date with both Conchita's findings and the task we had set Roma Bosch earlier that afternoon. Ferran was pleased. He and Maria had been involved all day in a fraud investigation involving the University and a leading manufacturing company in the city. It was important but very boring work they said, but this case was becoming very interesting.
"We will need to think carefully about how we progress this case. Hopefully your friend Roma will come up with the evidence that the Brotherhood owned properties in Bogatell and made a great deal of money selling them to the Olympic programme. We need to be careful though.

Solbes and his friends are very clever and very influential. Give me a while I will consider our actions from here." Ferran stated.
There was little more to do on the issue for the time being, Roma should have information for us tomorrow.

Ferran was suggesting he treat us all to tapas and wine at La Bombeta on Carrer de la Maquinista, just along from where we were. We were all ready for food and about to pay the bill for our drinks and move off when Kay remembered about the letter from Antich and Alvaro.
"This is really creepy," she said as she passed the letter over to Ferran
"These guys are dead and we get a letter from them."
Maria spoke for the first time:
"This must have been written before they died."
"That's obvious." replied Kay, "but it is still very spooky"
Ferran was surprisingly uninterested.
"There is more to this than we possibly think but now is not the time to discuss it. We are all hungry. Yes?" He asked. We all nodded.
"Then let's go."
Kay took back the letter and put it into my back pocket and we moved off towards La Bombeta.

It was late afternoon, early evening as the five of us moved off along Passeig Jean de Borbon on the way to La Bombeta. The evening was hot. The rains and thunder had moved off and the air was half way between the earlier cleanness and the usual sultriness. There was not a cloud in the sky. The streets were crowded and the atmosphere stank of summer and enjoyment. I felt about nineteen years old as I walked along with three very attractive women. I could tell from his behaviour that Ferran felt the same, as he, like me, had an extra little spring in his step, pleased to be seen and associated with such beauties.

La Bombeta was on Carrer La Maquinistsa, one of the main crossover streets in the grid of Barceloneta. The lower levels of all the apartment buildings were shops or restaurants. At this time of day the road was in the shade and more pleasantly cool because of it. La Bombeta was a favourite of the locals: Very cheap and cheerful, a good, cheap menu and wine by the jarra, at a basement price. At this time of the evening we could get a table fairly easily, but after nine p.m there would be no chance. We walked in and eased past the long food bar that ran the length of the main room, towards the twenty or so small tables that littered two-thirds of the eatery. We sat in the corner and, with the waiters help, pulled two tables together. The beers and wine arrived instantly and we looked over the Catalan menu. We decided on an array of tapas – bombas, patatas bravas, anchoas, pimientos, bacalao, chorizo, and several other varieties Kay and I hadn't tried before.

It wasn't long before our conversation returned to Julian Solbes.
Maria was the instigator:
"You see that Solbes is standing for Presidency de Catalonia in the election in three or four weeks time."
"Is he?" I added gormlessly.
"Si, he is favourite," commented Conchita.
"I would not vote for him if he were the only candidate and my mothers life depended on it," grumbled Ferran.
At that moment my mobile rang. I answered it.
"Hola, Steve Kenning."
"Steve. It is Roma. I have some information for you."
The others realised who it was and listened carefully. I pressed the speakerphone button on my mobile.
"Jaume has done well. He has copies of the deeds to thirteen properties owned by the Brotherhood with Julian Solbes as a signatory. These properties were later sold to

make way for Olympic village developments. They brought the properties only a matter of months before they sold them back in the 1980's. They sold them way above the price they paid for them. Even then they made several million pesetas, today the value would be many millions of euros."

"That's brilliant Roma, thank you very much. That's another meal we owe you!"

"No...no. It is my pleasure. The documents are at my office if you wish to collect them at some time. Adios."

"Great." I said.

"We must nearly have the man."

"Yes. We must continue to play this carefully, especially with the election nearly upon us. Otherwise, people might just see it as a nother political attempt to discredit him," added Ferran.

A really loud ring from Ferran's phone surprised us.

"Digame."

He looked concerned as he listened intently to the voice on the line.

"No. No, este impossible." He listened again.

"No, no soy....." The voice was louder on the other end of the line.

After a few minutes Ferran relented with a: "Vale, vale."

Ferran slammed the phone down on the table. We all looked at him for an explanation.

"They want me to go to Valencia. They want me to investigate a plot to murder one of the candidates for the Presidency. They say I need to spend two or three weeks there." He looked forlorn.

"They want you out of the way," stated Maria.

"Si, they want more time to cover their tracks. We have obviously got far too close."

"Do you have to go?" enquired Kay naively.

"Si, I must. I would never work in the city again if I refused."

"What do we do now then?" I questioned.
"Well, Conchita can get all the evidence together but I am sure they will find ways to discredit it over the next few weeks. Maria is to go with me – orders." He looked across to her. She was obviously cross at leaving this case but pleased to be going with Ferran.

We took a few minutes to discuss Ferran and Maria's task in Valencia. They were very cross, but resigned to the job they had been given. Ferran stood up and glared at Kay and I.
"You two….." He looked at us as he and Maria prepared to leave.
"You two….enjoy your holiday. I hope to see you in a couple of weeks time." With that they kissed us both and Conchita and left us to our beers.

Chapter Thirty Two

Self-satisfaction

Autosatisfacción

It's a great feeling when you complete a job or a task to a really high level of quality. The feeling of satisfaction is rarely matched. The feeling is particularly enhanced when you have done something that has involved an element of deception that has gone unnoticed. Some people live their lives deceiving others, often very successfully. Such success can lead to smugness and self-satisfaction. When such attitudes are followed by complacency there is often a good chance that the deceiver will be trapped.

August 19th 2005, 3.30 p.m – Can Pixho Restaurant, Barceloneta

The restaurant inhabited by an assorted purely male company felt almost as it had almost thirty years ago. The restaurant, although of the same name, was an extremely different affair to its earlier namesake. Instead of the low ceilinged cavernous brick walled room of 30 years ago that was low on style and quality, yet high on space, atmosphere and character, they were assembled on the first floor of the plush restaurant, full of all the latest comforts that were designed to make the paying customer comfortable – air conditioning, subdued lighting, roomy, clean toilets. The new location was perched at the very edge of the Barceloneta grid of buildings, with a view across the esplanade onto the beach. The view covered the near exact location of the old Can Pixho chiringuito restaurant that had strewn its way across where the beach now was. The new Can Pixho was one of the more expensive and refined restaurants that now fronted the maritime edge of Barceloneta. It was a long way from the old days of the chiringuito that had held the romance of being a real local institution, always busy, particularly at weekends and on public holidays when the Barcelonans would flood the maritime zone. Today Can Pixho had its fair share of Catalan customers but the real money was made from the tourists who now flocked to Barcelona and in particular the coastline. The re-invention of the city as a result of the 1992 Olympics had been remarkably successful in every respect, but in particular in bringing a real wealth to the city.

The restaurant had been rearranged in respect of its honoured guests. The pale yellow walls were more evident as the normally spaced out tables had either been removed or placed together so that one long, large table could take centre stage in the room. Half-lit, half circle pottery wall lights hugged the pale walls, providing enough light on this late summer afternoon. The room glowed with the pale tiled floor shining in the light of the wall lamps and the white tablecloth lighting up the faces of the men seated around it.

Thirty years is a long time and the faces of the men told a series of many stories. The last time they had sat around in this way was as a group of aspiring and forward thinking young men, full of apprehensions about an uncertain future, but also full of expectant hope for the life that stretched out ahead of them. Now this group of older men still displayed some of that hope and expectancy but only in isolated areas. The men wore their life experiences and their life attitudes on their faces. Invariably it was those who still had the vibrancy of life and hopes for the future that looked better. The physical condition of the assembly of men was varied in the extreme, ranging from Julian Solbes, who although he was now 58, he looked to be in his early forties, with an everlasting tan, perfect teeth, a full head of hair and a perfect body for a man of half his age, to Manuel Perez, who had a thin strip of grey, nearly white hair that skirted the base of his skull which sat partially covered by a vast neck that swallowed up the collar of his shirt and very nearly his chin. He was virtually immobile and his 23 stone of blubber had to be pushed up the stairs of the restaurant by two waiters. The exertion had obviously been too much for him as he sat quietly in the room, pale and sweating heavily.

Can Pixho, all those years ago, had seen the official formation of La Hermandad de la Noveno Noviembre. Then there were 12 young men, eager to form a bond for personal and financial security. Today there were 7 survivors. Survivors who had made it through the turbulent post-Franco years and had together amassed a substantial wealth as a result of shrewd investments in the growth and prosperity, of their city, of Barcelona. Solbes and Perez were joined, around the table, by Xavier Badia, Salvador Camps, Raul Martinez, Rafael Gastesi and Jose Baquero. The others were all dead.

Unlike thirty years ago there was no gulf between the men with confidence and leadership qualities and those young men who were careful of what they said and how they said it. The petty rivalries of thirty years ago were gone. The seven men were each very wealthy and very successful. Not all had stayed in the financial world but they each had a well-developed personality and character, independent of others. It was Solbes though who stood up first. He was very confident that he would soon be elected President of the Catalonian Government, at a time when the region was beginning to gain increasing independence from Spain. He was a shrewd politician and had played a very important part in the revitalisation of Barcelona and the continued economic development of the Catalan region over the past 10 years. His business and political dealings, along with his marriage to Maquista Peragell, the daughter of the President of Banco Sabadona and perhaps the richest man in the region, had also brought him considerable wealth and a lifestyle to match. He now lived mostly on his multi-million pound yacht moored conspicuously in the heart of the Port Vell marina, at other times he took residence at his presidential style quarters in the hills above the city. He looked and behaved like a film star. The almost President elect and his wife were regulars at parties, banquets, openings of galleries, and anywhere where they might get their pictures taken for any of the glossy gossip magazines that abound in Spain.

He stood as the conversation lulled in the room. He raised his glass in his right hand. He sipped the classic Cava from his glass.

"Ahh." He smiled and looked at the contents of his glass which he now held at arms length.

"This wonderful country of ours has served us well. Where better in the world could we be? We have the best wines, the best food, sunshine, culture to create envy in the world, a vibrant economy, we grow most of our own food, and the women…"

He smiled again and raised both his eyebrows to the delight of the other

six men who all smiled and giggled in agreement.

"…and not forgetting the mighty F.C. Barca."

At this point the seven men simultaneously broke into a chant of "Barca, Barca, Barca," whilst clapping and stamping their feet. After a couple of minutes this subsided and the other six men looked back towards Solbes.

"Before we continue…"
He looked at the table and placed his glass down and clasped his hands in front of him.
"…we must pay respect to our partners, our friends, our members of the Brotherhood who did not make it this far."
The others rose from their chairs to stand in respect. Perez was struggling to get a grip on the sides of the flimsy chair that was miraculously supporting his incredible weight.
"Not you Manuel." blurted out Solbes,
"You need to rest."
With that a relieved Perez slumped back into his chair. With most of the assembled group now standing, Solbes continued.
"We are a Brotherhood and we have all benefited enormously, personally and financially, from our allegiance. We could not have achieved anything alone. Each and everyone of the Brotherhood have played their part in what has been a quite magnificently successful and complex venture. We, those of us here today, have a long life ahead of us."
Solbes glanced around the room, quickly passing over Perez.
"That life will continue to be good through the fruits of our combined efforts. We have much to thank our departed brothers." He paused, apparently, deep in thought.
"To the Brotherhood!" Solbes raised his glass again and was joined by the others in saluting their allegiance.

The group settled back down into their seats. Now was the time to talk openly and as a group. It was the first time they had met openly in this way for a long time. Xavier Badia spoke out to the group.

"The operations we put in place in the first few years of the Brotherhood and the subsequent formation of Hermandad, S.A, our public limited company, were extremely fortuitous and timely. At any other time in any other place the opportunities to do what we did would not have been possible."

Badia, now the owner of a large successful firm of solicitors, had been the overall financial brain behind the early operations of the Brotherhood. Despite his portly frame, bald-head and Hitchcock like features, his exuberant personality and his expensive grooming made him not an unduly unattractive character. Badia was full of energy and was constantly on the move. He ate and drank constantly which, but for his perpetual motion, would have put him in the same size league as the unfortunate Perez. Instead, Badia, was as fit and healthy as the best of the rest of the Brotherhood. You could just tell from his demeanour and manner that he was going to live a long time. Badia didn't reveal what all the Brotherhood knew. They had been lucky in that there had been a certain amount of confusion following the death of Franco in the late nineteen seventies, as the new Spanish sovereign nation laid its foundations across a very shaky landscape. The Brotherhood had used their positions to borrow state money to invest in land and subsequently property development in the Poble Nou and Bogatell areas of the city. This area had been the industrial powerhouse of the city, although by the end of the 1970's many of the factories had closed or were used as warehouses. Solbes had become active politically and he had stumbled on the plans for developing the old industrial areas that were next to both the sea and the city centre, as part of an ambitious plan to revitalise the city and to win the bid for the 1992 Olympics. With this information the Brotherhood used the borrowed funds to invest in a large area of virtually unwanted cheap land, which they knew would shortly be sought after. They made a great amount of money from this deal. They carefully repaid the state and invested the rest in other larger pockets of land in the same area forming a legal property development company, Hermandad S.A. The only really illegal thing they had done was to use money that belonged to the state, even though it was only ever meant to be a loan. The methods and strategies used to transfer money to buy and sell property were extremely clever and virtually untraceable as the Brotherhood often used the names of government organisations. The Brotherhood also used their knowledge and influence to shape their fortunes. Despite all the dealings that took place the Brotherhood was never implicated.

"Who would have guessed…" continued Badia, now having gained everyone's attention.

"…that a football team, albeit full of very clever, unusually, footballers, could achieve what we have achieved. What we did in those early days was not illegal, although had we made a mistake, I doubt we would be here now…"

The group chuckled nervously in agreement.

"…but it was very clever. In the past thirty years it was only earlier this year when there was any doubt of us being successful. We have supported Julian and his political influence has helped our cause. But had there been any kind of exposure with or without real evidence of our dealings it would have created a scandal that would almost certainly have ended his political hopes…and we would all have suffered then." Rafael Gestasi butted in.

"I quite enjoyed it when you, me and Baquero died and came back to life again."

The men laughed at the image he had conveyed. Baquero joined in.

"That was a very clever smokescreen you created Xavier."

Badia shook his head.

"It was not my idea. Anything to do with public relations or how we handle situations has always been the work of Manuel (Perez) and Raul (Martinez). Their public relations skills have helped them create the biggest advertising agency in Southern Europe and have managed Julian's political campaigns very successfully over the years. They must take the credit."

At this point Perez started to glow. Whatever his physical state he had a fine brain and great intuition. He always knew how to handle situations. "Always think what the others are thinking and then think of something different." The words bellowed out from inside the huge man. His partner for the past twenty or so years, Raul Martinez, looked across at Perez with a mixture of real affection and concern for his partner and friend. 'Mano" as he called Perez, "is the brains, I just put his ideas into operation." You could see that these two were the perfect partnership. Perez had nothing else in his life to do other than sit around and use that very clever tool of his, his brain. He had always liked to think even in his younger, thinner days. He was a loner and counted Martinez as his only real friend and his only family. Martinez on the other hand was a slim, trim figure of a man in his late fifties. He had Arab blood and this was revealed in his dark skin and full head of slicked back black hair. There were no traces of grey anywhere on his head except for at the base of his short sideburns and intermittently in his neat, small moustache. He was wearing a bright plain tangerine matching shirt and tie which, along with his expensive royal blue mohair suit, made him look easily the most flamboyant and exotic of the assorted company. He even made Solbes look conservative in his dress.

"We felt that if we created a smoke screen and involved the police that there was nothing to really investigate and the issue would quietly blow away. Certain mistakes had been made by members of the Brotherhood at this time, and we had to act quickly. It may have been a mistaken approach but it worked."

As Martinez spoke there was a short hush as they reflected on the mistakes. "Badia had made a serious error in letting 'his' son know about the Brotherhood. Antich and Alvero had played their part in spreading the incredible story of the actions of the Brotherhood – we knew the police would not believe it and could never prove it, although they acted on their own instincts taking actions which could have horribly backfired on the Brotherhood, instead of playing it steady as instructed. They always were out for excitement, still it was a real pity they died in such a terrible and untimely accident."

Salvador Camps had kept reasonably quiet so far. He was a big man. His grey thinning hair was swept back across his head. He wore a black leather jacket, black shirt and a white tie. Gold jangled on his wrists. He wore sunglasses everywhere. No one could remember what colour his eyes were. His love was art and he owned and ran a number of private galleries around the city. With the exception of Solbes he was the most influential. He was a master at quiet diplomacy and quiet politics. He knew everyone and he could make anything happen in Barcelona. He fiddled with the base of his empty glass. He had sensed the changing atmosphere of the meeting, feeling that accusations, recriminations and other long held debts were about to surface.

"All I am interested in is the sparkling wine. My glass is empty."

He grouched accusingly. Badia, who was sitting next to him, picked up a bottle of Cava and refilled his glass.

"Thank you Xavier. Now all I am interested in….." he paused to take a sip of cava."…is the future. Enough of

the past. From this moment on there is nothing but the future."
Everyone nodded in agreement.
"The Brotherhood has served us well for thirty years. I see no reason to change. We have a very successful company which helps all of us, including me, to live the life we wish to live and indulge in our passions."
In Camps case it was women, art, women, women, art and F.C Barcelona, roughly in that order.
"We have had a very pleasant meal this afternoon, shared stories and some secrets…we have had fun. Have we not?"
No one could disagree. They all nodded, muttered their agreement and drank cava.
"We have lost five out of 12 of us over thirty years. That, according to my mental capacity, which after the amount of cava I have drunk this afternoon, is not great, is about one death every 8 years. I suggest therefore that we meet again in this way, at this time, every five years. In that way at least two of us should meet in 2045!"
No one was up to the maths involved in this calculation so instead they all nodded in agreement. La Hermandad del Noveno Noviembre continued their meeting satisfied with what they had collectively achieved.

Chapter Thirty-Three

Justice

Justicia

Everyone is involved in illegal activity at some point or other. At the lowest level it may be simply utilising someone else's wireless channel with your computer, or even to the level of walking off with the complementary newspaper in a café. Proportionally though few of us take things much further. Only a small percentage of the population of any area engage in cynically, pre-planned crime. What is surprising is that a substantial number of this small percentage of people are outwardly successful and powerful. Maybe it is because they are calculating, immoral and devious that they are able to fully utilise their criminal tendencies and activities to achieve success. Whatever, to those of us who do have higher moral standards than these low life, it is immensely satisfying when they receive what they are all eventually likely to get – justice.

August 19th 2005, 4 p.m – Can Pixho Restaurant, Barceloneta

La Hermandad del Noveno Noviembre was enjoying its successes. A large amount of alcohol had been consumed, by the seven remaining members, gathered on this August afternoon, in the Can Pixho restaurant. The sun had come out from behind the earlier overcast skies and fresh sunlight was flooding into the first floor restaurant through the windows that provided a stunning view over the beach and sea. The mood of the room was positive and relaxed. Small private conversations were going on between the seven men who were sat around the table.

The mood of each of the seven Brotherhood members was so mellow and relaxed that no-one noticed as a further seven people shuffled into the room and assembled at the far end of the long restaurant. The visitors stood watching and listening.

Eventually one of the watchers stepped forward. At this point the members of the Brotherhood gradually noticed him and the other interlopers. One by one they stopped their conversations and turned to face the uninvited.
"Julian Solbes, esta aqui?"
Julian Solbes slowly raised his hand to signify his presence. He said nothing. Everyone looked at the seven people at the far end of the restaurant. Five of them were armed, uniformed officers of the Mossos d'Esquadra.
"Julian Solbes?" Repeated the main man.
"You are to accompany us to the offices of the Mossos d'Esquadra as you are to be charged with the murder of Jordi Torras, the attempted murder of Jesus Antich and Jose Lluis Alvaro, and the misuse of position, power and government funds to your own ends."
There was silence.

Slowly everyone in the room turned to look towards the reaction of Julian Solbes. There was an atmosphere of disbelief in the room. The other members of the Brotherhood were agog. All eyes were on Solbes. His previous arrogance and swagger could be seen to be visibly ebbing away from his persona. This was an untouchable, very successful and powerful man. How could anyone have the audacity to question his authority or, even worse, accuse him of such terrible crimes? It was plain from his expression that these had been his first thoughts as soon as Detective Ferran had laid out the accusations. Like any good politician though, Solbes had thought quickly before he spoke. He soon realised that no one would come to this public meeting and make such accusations unless they had real evidence to back up their statements. The resignation ran through his face like a man who had gambled everything on a losing number on a roulette wheel. He knew that his good life had come to an end.

Solbes stood up slowly and in silence. As he began to move towards Ferran and the other awaiting police, Xavier Badia grabbed his hand and quietly said,
"Julian no. They are wrong. Fight them, fight them."
His words were hollow as he too could see the resignation that haunted Solbes's eyes. He had always hoped he would not be caught out but he had always one day expected to be made to pay for his crimes. He was older now, but no wiser. He did though want to pay some dues for his crimes. His manner suggested this and he quickly released Badias grip and walked serenely over towards the police. Two of the uniformed officers handcuffed him and escorted him down the stairs. Ferran remained rooted to his spot. He hadn't finished with the Brotherhood yet. He was really enjoying himself. This could be the pinnacle of his career, not that that interested him at all. However this was a real accomplishment on his part. Not only had he caught out one of the cleverest and most cynical criminals in Catalonia, he had also managed to find a route around all the political connections that Solbes had in order to make this arrest. Ferran was growing in stature as he stood over the remaining six seated members of the Brotherhood. He felt ten feet tall. His long black jacket was open and flowing, framing his crisp white shirt, unbuttoned at the neck.

He had now been joined by Maria. Who had moved away from the three remaining Mossos officers. Ferran continued.

"Xavier Badia you will also accompany us to the offices of the Mossos d'Esquadra. You are charged with the attempted murder of Antich and Alavaro, and assisting in the murder of Jordi Torras, and the embezzlement of public funds."
Badia too had seen this coming after Solbes had left the room. He had shrunk to a tiny man as he got up and stumbled out of the restaurant with the support of a couple of officers.

The remaining five members of the Brotherhood were still completely bemused. For the past five minutes not one of them had said a word and not one of them could believe what was happening. They had been led for nearly thirty years by their charismatic and indefatigable leader who now was under arrest. There was no doubt in their minds about their successes and his leadership. In a matter of minutes their world had been totally re-interpreted for them. Ferran once more addressed his captive audience.
"Gentlemen." He paused for effect. He was really beginning to enjoy himself.
"You are all implicated in the dealings of La Hermandad del Noveno Noviembre. We have many more investigations to undertake. As you will appreciate some of the situations we need to look into took place nearly thirty years ago. You will all be expected to assist us with our investigations. Whilst these are undertaken you will all be expected to remain in Catalonia. Thank you."

As he ended a groan came from the far end of the table. Manuel Perez had looked dreadful all afternoon. His huge bulk had been fragilely contained in a flimsy chair. The groan though was followed by the collapse of the chair as his body flopped to his right. Suddenly the whole chair had collapsed with the hulk of his body sent crashing to the floor. He groaned and held his chest. This had been just too much for him. Ferran instructed the three uniformed officers to help him. An ambulance was called for and within minutes', two, stretcher bearing paramedics, had appeared from the hospital that was located right next door to the restaurant. Perez was still alive but only just, as he was taken out of the restaurant.

Ferran looked around at the dismal reflection of all the intrigue, hard work, criminal activity, and murder that the Brotherhood had been either fully knowing of or accepting of over the past thirty years. All this, for what? Four shattered, probably generally innocent, men stayed rooted to their chairs. They were quietly discussing anything they could remember that had made it all go wrong. Ferran and Maria took a last long look at the room, smiled at each other and then headed out of that sad place.

Chapter Thirty-Four

Absolute Bliss

Dicha Absoluta

I never wish I was younger because I am now what I have become because of the experiences I have had in life, but when I sit on the beach in Barcelona I do wonder what I might get up to if I was twenty years younger. I am sure there are many cities with beaches, but I have never been on a beach with as many distractingly gorgeous women as those on Barcelona beach. The view then was excellent, the sunshine and blue sky perfect and in abundance, the continual refreshment of a bottle or can of Estrella Damm was exquisite and the company, my beautiful wife Kay, was unbeatable. Absolute bliss.

August 20th 2005, 4 p.m – San Sebastian Beach, Barceloneta

The past few weeks had been extremely relaxing and the memories of the events that engulfed Kay and I during the first days of our summer holiday seemed far distant. When Ferran and Maria left La Bombeta on August 2nd that had been the last we had seen of them. We hadn't even seen Conchita who had been left behind in Barcelona. It had taken us a few days to relax and not to be continually looking over our shoulders and suspecting everyone we meet of some kind of subterfuge, but we had managed it. Our daily routine was lazy, but well deserved in our view. Get up late, coffee and croissant in our favourite cheap café, wander around the streets for an hour or so, hit the beach for four or five hours, a few beers, then eat either at home or more often than not at a cheap, local, restaurant. I looked across at Kay. She had gone a beautiful bronze colour. She was laid out on her back on top of a towel on the sandy beach reading a Robert Wilson novel. She looked lovely. I often looked at her wondering what on earth she was doing with me. I enjoyed the vista of beauties on the beach but my eyes always came back to the lovely Kay.

It was now late afternoon and I was enjoying my book. The only problem with the beach in Barceloneta was that it could get extremely crowded and when it did people walked right by you sometimes kicking up sand. Exactly that was happening right now. Sand was being showered over me and Kay. We both sat up in indignation. I had my most annoyed look on my face, ready to enforce my feelings towards the culprit.

"Ferran. Maria," howled Kay and quickly stood up to hug them both. I got to my feet and hugged the beautiful Maria. She was dressed in an orange and brown bikini with a matching wrap. She looked like a film star. Ferran and I shook hands warmly. He was also dressed for the beach with his surf shorts.

"How are you both?" he asked.

"We are fine. Life has been less exciting since you left but we are well relaxed," replied Kay.

"You both look very well. Mucho bueno!" added Maria.

"Do you want a drink?" I asked.

They both nodded, so Kay and I picked up our towels and books, rammed them into our beach bag and headed for the nearest beach bar. There were two tables free right on the beach. We sat down and attracted the waitresses' attention for four beers.

Ferran and Maria looked increasingly good together. They looked tired but very satisfied. We now knew Ferran well enough to understand him a little.

"Why are you looking so smug?" I asked Ferran.

He was leaning back in his chair. He looked at Maria and they both smiled. Then he leant towards us.

"Well. You know that little problem we were working on before we were called to Valencia? Well it has all been resolved."

"What problem?" asked Kay.

"Not the Julian Solbes problem?"

"Si, exactamente!"

"Wow, how?" Drooled Kay, eager for information.

"It is quite a long story, but you need to know. I will tell you."

He took a sip from the glass the waitress had just placed in front of him.

"As you know, we had a lot of information about the operation of the Brotherhood and in particular the dirty dealings of Solbes and Badia in relation to property development. This was really good stuff, although it was never going to be enough to put Solbes in the place he deserves to be."

"Where's that?" I asked.

"In prison for life." replied Maria.

Ferran continued, "Something you didn't know is that Josep Lluis Alvaro and Jesus Antich didn't die in that accident the night they left you at La Portes 7."

"How? What?" said an amazed Kay.

"Yes. I was surprised. They were taken from the scene of the accident unconscious and badly injured. I was told that they were dead, as I could not get to see them to interview them. Instead, Antich had come round fairly soon after the accident and ordered one of the doctors to immediately arrange for them to be transferred to a private clinic deep in the Pyrenees. Unfortunately, he did this but didn't tell the hospital administration who promptly announced they were dead. Anyway, we soon discovered a number of deliberate faults on their car that had almost certainly led to the accident. We tracked down the people that did the damage to the car. More of this later."

He paused for another drink.

"Anyway. About nine days ago, I had a call from the Jefe of the criminal justice system in the whole of Catalonia, Ricardo Lluis Manresa. .....a very important man. Most importantly not a fan or a friend of Julian Solbes. Senor Manresa had been in contact with Antich and Alvaro and they had provided him with a great amount of incriminating information about Julian Solbes and Xavier Badia. I was called immediately up to his house in Girona."

This was interesting. Kay and I were hooked, we hadn't even touched our drinks.

"When I got to Girona, which by the way is a long way from Valencia, Antich and Alvaro were at Senor Manresa's house. They were not perfect but they had been patched together pretty well. We met for several hours, Antich, Alvaro, Senor Manresa, Maria and me. The information the two men had was irrefutable. They took us way back to the start of the Brotherhood and they filled us in on all the dealings that they knew about, and the methods they had used. A great deal of it was not illegal, just very, very clever. In fact the majority of the members of the Brotherhood, apart from temporarily borrowing government funds, had seemingly done nothing wrong. Things though started to full apart with the Brotherhood some years ago, at a time when Solbes started to have serious political ambitions. He was implicated in a potential financial scandal, as he had used his position and links to make money from the property dealings of the Brotherhood. A few members of the Brotherhood were less than supportive to Solbes. He and Badia, his sidekick had them killed."

"How do know this?" I asked.

"Surely you need more that the word of two bitter men?"

"Ahh. Yes. But Antich and Alvaro told us who did the work for Solbes and Badia. They had investigated Solbes very thoroughly themselves and had found the killers and had their testimonies. We checked these out, found the people involved. In return for some leniency on their sentences they provided us with more details, admitted their crimes, implicated Solbes and also admitted to the attempted murder of Antich and Alavaro."

"So you had more than enough to get Solbes?" agreed Kay.

"Yes, but I haven't told you the best bit yet." said a smiling Ferran.

We both looked at him, our eyes begging him to tell us more.

"Antich had a computer memory stick. He showed it to us that night in Girona. I couldn't believe it. It showed, very clearly Solbes and Badia with Jordi Torras when he died earlier this summer. When we first met. Remember? The video clip showed Solbes murder Jordi Torras in a fit of temper."

"Christ," I said as Kay looked at Ferran open mouthed.

"So you see we had a great amount of evidence. Yesterday, as a result of all this new evidence we arrested Solbes and Badia in that restaurant over there."

Ferran pointed towards the Can Pixto restaurant just across from the beach.

"Have you not seen the news today? It is all over the newspapers and TV?"

"Wow, no….so what did Solbes say?" Kay asked.

"He admitted absolutely everything. I couldn't believe it. He is still going now, telling his story to our officers."

Ferran continued to give us more stories related to this great arrest. He and Maria were quite delighted. The joy radiated from their faces and they glowed with satisfaction. We made plans to celebrate later that evening at the elegant restaurant Pla. This was going to be a great evening. Kay squeezed my hand lovingly at the side of the table and looked at me with a beautiful smile. Ferran decided we were to celebrate with the essence of life itself – Cava! He ordered a bottle as we soaked up the sun. Life doesn't get much better!

Printed in the United Kingdom
by Lightning Source UK Ltd.
120146UK00001B/26

9 781846 853074